Saraswati Nagpal

DRAUPADI

The fire-born princess

CAMPFIRE®

KALYANI NAVYUG MEDIA PVT LTD

Draupadi
The fire-born princess

Script
Saraswati Nagpal

Content Development and Research
Neelam Bhatt

Edits
Parama Majumder

Line Art
Manu

Color
Pradeep Sherawat
Vijay Sharma

Desktop Publishing
Bhavnath Chaudhary

CAMPFIRE®
www.campfire.co.in

Mission Statement

To entertain and educate young minds by creating unique illustrated books
that recount stories of human values, arouse curiosity in the world around us,
and inspire with tales of great deeds of unforgettable people.

Published by Kalyani Navyug Media Pvt Ltd
101 C, Shiv House, Hari Nagar Ashram, New Delhi 110014, India

ISBN: 978-93-80741-09-3

Printed in India

About the Author

Since she can remember, Saraswati has been in love with words. As a child, her appetite for books was insatiable. She took to writing as a young girl, planning her first book when she was ten years old, though she only managed one chapter back then. She wrote plays, stories, and poems through high school and college.

Saraswati is also an educator who believes in fun classrooms and joyful learning. All the children she teaches and meets inspire her to retell old stories and make up magical new ones.

Other than writing, she adores dancing, animals, and the colour purple.

A bit of a world traveller, Saraswati has lived in Dubai, Delhi, and Fairfield, Iowa. She currently spends her time between mystical India and beautiful South Africa.

In Vedic lore, Saraswati is the serene goddess of speech, art, and wisdom. Saraswati is very glad to be named after her.

Saraswati's first published work, the Campfire graphic novel *Sita: Daughter of the Earth*, was the first Indian mythological graphic novel to be shortlisted for the Stan Lee Excelsior Award (2012).

The Kuru Family Tree

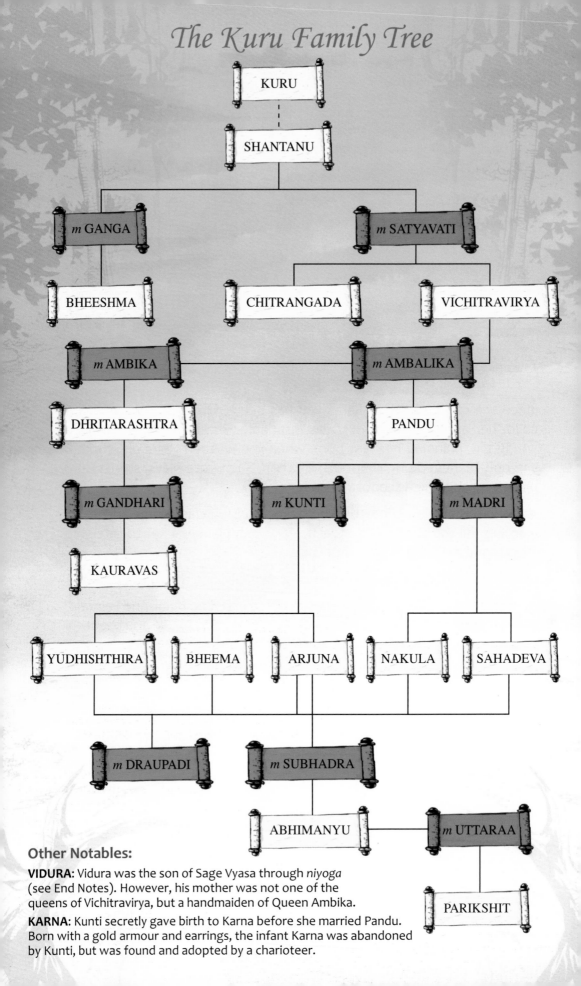

Other Notables:

VIDURA: Vidura was the son of Sage Vyasa through *niyoga* (see End Notes). However, his mother was not one of the queens of Vichitravirya, but a handmaiden of Queen Ambika.

KARNA: Kunti secretly gave birth to Karna before she married Pandu. Born with a gold armour and earrings, the infant Karna was abandoned by Kunti, but was found and adopted by a charioteer.

Here sits the great storyteller Maharishi* Vyasa. The story he writes unfolded in Bhaaratvarsha**, a land blessed by the gods.

It was a magical age called Dwapara Yuga, when the gods and their children took mortal form; when men and women lived extraordinary lives and became the legendary heroes that people would tell stories about.

It was a time when people looked up to Kshatriyas, the warrior class, as their protectors. But filled with greed, many of them misused their power to terrorise those they were meant to protect. To amass wealth, they fought their noble brothers, killed them mercilessly, and showed no respect for life. The earth was heavy with sorrow for their evil deeds.

It was during this age that a prophecy foretold of the destruction of these evil warriors. To cause this destruction and fulfil the prophecy, one woman arose from the sacred fire.

I am that woman. My name is Draupadi.

Born in an age when women were appreciated for their patience and sweetness, they say that my thoughts burnt bright as flames, and my words were sharp like fire-tipped arrows.

Perhaps it is true – I would like to think it is. But you, dear reader, may decide for yourself. For here is my story...

*An illustrious and highly venerated sage

**Another name for India

5

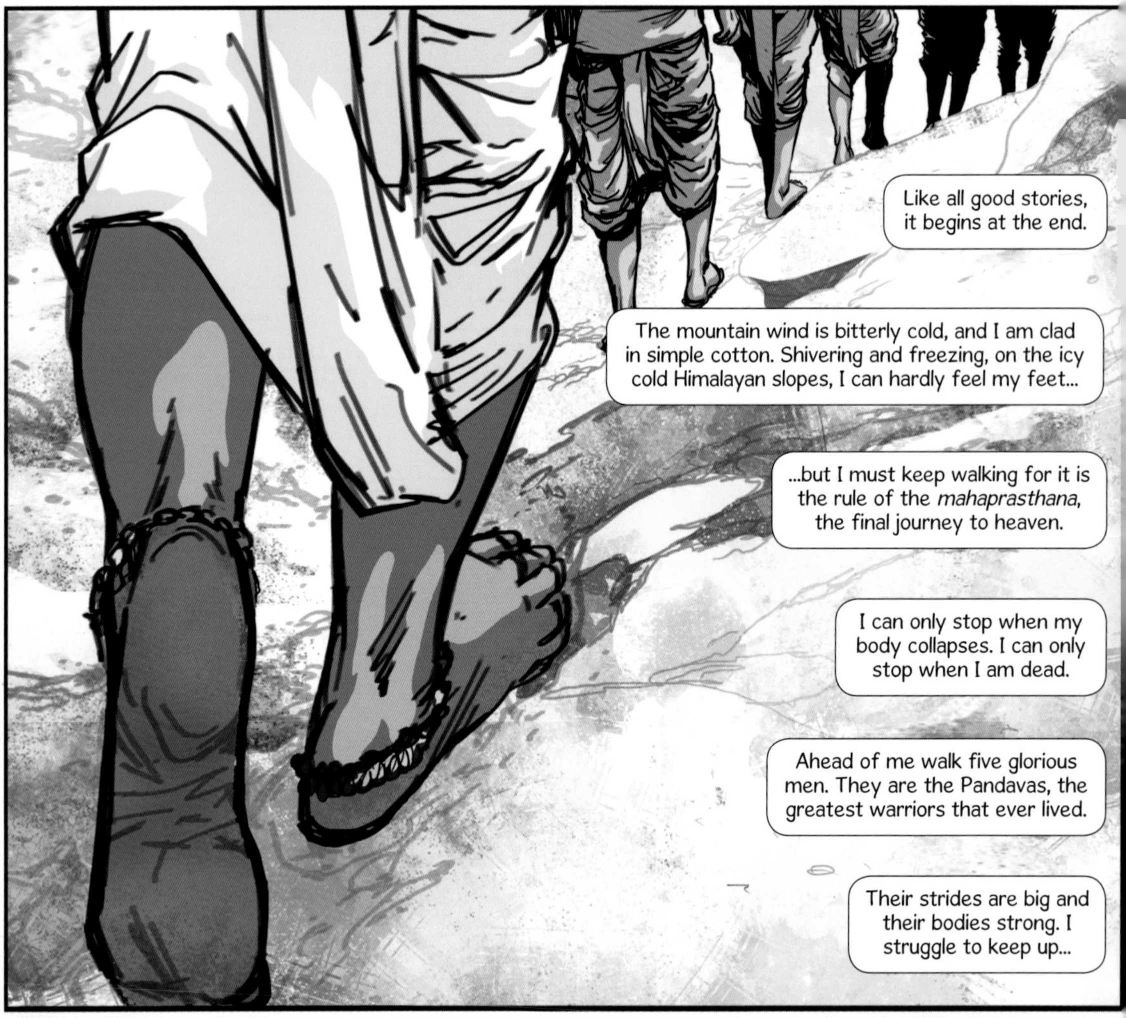
Like all good stories, it begins at the end.
The mountain wind is bitterly cold, and I am clad in simple cotton. Shivering and freezing, on the icy cold Himalayan slopes, I can hardly feel my feet...
...but I must keep walking for it is the rule of the *mahaprasthana*, the final journey to heaven.
I can only stop when my body collapses. I can only stop when I am dead.
Ahead of me walk five glorious men. They are the Pandavas, the greatest warriors that ever lived.
Their strides are big and their bodies strong. I struggle to keep up...

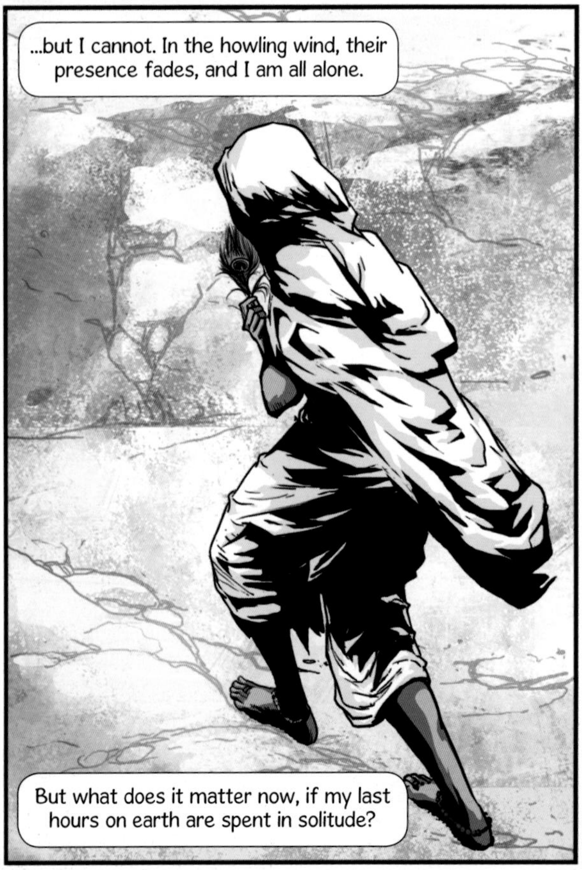
...but I cannot. In the howling wind, their presence fades, and I am all alone.
But what does it matter now, if my last hours on earth are spent in solitude?

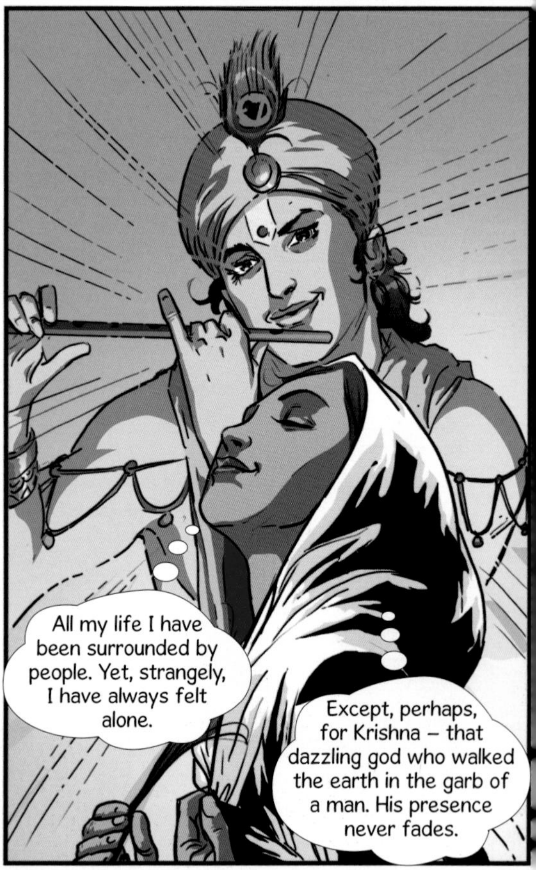
All my life I have been surrounded by people. Yet, strangely, I have always felt alone.
Except, perhaps, for Krishna – that dazzling god who walked the earth in the garb of a man. His presence never fades.

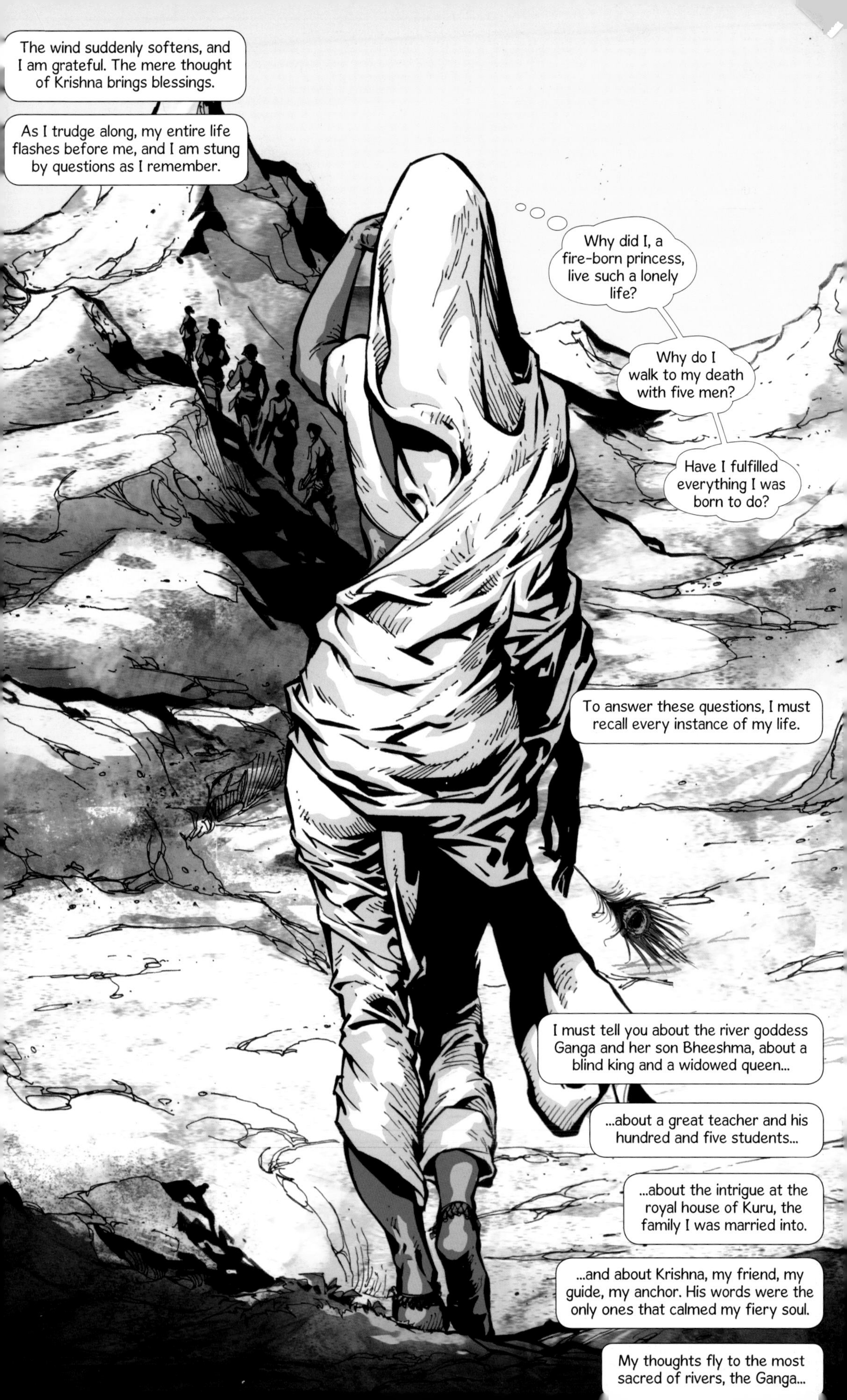
The wind suddenly softens, and I am grateful. The mere thought of Krishna brings blessings.
As I trudge along, my entire life flashes before me, and I am stung by questions as I remember.
Why did I, a fire-born princess, live such a lonely life?
Why do I walk to my death with five men?
Have I fulfilled everything I was born to do?
To answer these questions, I must recall every instance of my life.
I must tell you about the river goddess Ganga and her son Bheeshma, about a blind king and a widowed queen...
...about a great teacher and his hundred and five students...
...about the intrigue at the royal house of Kuru, the family I was married into.
...and about Krishna, my friend, my guide, my anchor. His words were the only ones that calmed my fiery soul.
My thoughts fly to the most sacred of rivers, the Ganga...

Devavrata was born of Ganga and King Shantanu of the Kuru dynasty that ruled the kingdom of Hastinapur.

But Satyavati's father objected to the marriage. He was worried that the throne of Hastinapur would rightfully pass to Devavrata after Shantanu died. This meant that Satyavati's children would have no chance of becoming rulers.

To put the fisherman's fears to rest, Devavrata took a terrible oath.

When Devavrata was still very young, Ganga left him and Shantanu to return to her river abode, and the king grieved for many years.

One day, while hunting in the woods, Shantanu met Satyavati, the beautiful daughter of a fisherman, and fell in love with her.

Devavrata persuaded his father, the king, to marry Satyavati and make her the new queen.

8

Invoking the gods as witness, Devavrata renounced his right to the throne of Hastinapur forever. He also vowed that he would never marry and would never have children of his own.

The gods were amazed at the courage of this sixteen-year-old prince who had sacrificed power and pleasure for his father's sake. From the heavens, they gave him a new name, **Bheeshma**, the one who took inviolable oaths.

Bheeshma remained a loyal caretaker of the throne, lovingly tending to his half-brothers.

Thus, the only successors to the Kuru throne were now Satyavati's children and grandchildren.

Satyavati had two sons with Shantanu – Chitrangada and Vichitravirya.

But tragedy struck twice. His half-brothers died young. Chitrangada left no heirs, but Vichitravirya's queens gave birth to a son each...

Dhritarashtra, the eldest son of Vichitravirya, was born blind. But he was blessed with extraordinary strength in his arms. It was said that he could crush a statue of iron by simply embracing it.

But a blind man cannot rule a kingdom, so the throne went to his younger brother, Pandu. Dhritarashtra secretly resented this.

Strong as a lion, Pandu was a handsome and mighty warrior with a kind heart. He made a good king for Hastinapur, and dearly loved his blind brother.

He did not see the bitterness in Dhritarashtra's heart.

The two princes had a half-brother called Vidura. He was wise and gentle, and famous for his honesty and humility. He studied politics, law, and philosophy, and was made Chief Advisor to Pandu.

He was considered the most learned member of the royal court.

Dhritarashtra married **Gandhari**, the beautiful princess of Gandhar. Out of love for her husband, Gandhari blindfolded herself with a silk sash, promising to live in darkness for the rest of her life, just as he would.

The couple had one hundred sons and one daughter, Dushala. The sons of Dhritarashtra were known as the **Kauravas**, the eldest of whom was Duryodhana, followed by Dushasana.

Even as children, the Kauravas were vain, arrogant, and selfish.

They were doted upon and pampered by Gandhari's brother, Prince Shakuni, a sly man and an expert in the game of dice.

He spent most of his time in Hastinapur and encouraged his nephews, especially Duryodhana and Dushasana, to act with deceit.

Shakuni believed that it was Duryodhana's destiny to be the king of Hastinapur. He reminded Duryodhana every day that as long as Pandu and his sons were alive, Duryodhana would never have the kingdom to himself.

Carefully, Shakuni fostered the little Kaurava's hatred for the sons of Pandu.

King Pandu married princesses **Kunti** and **Madri**. They were beautiful and wise women, and shared their husband's good nature and kindness.

But fate took a cruel turn for Pandu. He was cursed into celibacy for accidently killing a sage and his wife. Relinquishing his crown, he retired to the forest with Kunti and Madri.

The two women prayed to the gods, who gifted them sons with celestial powers. These boys, the sons of Pandu, were called the **Pandavas**.

The eldest was **Yudhishthira**, gifted to Kunti by Dharma, the god of righteousness. He was honest, just, and wise.

Vayu, the wind god, granted Kunti a son named **Bheema**. He had superhuman strength, but a soft and kind heart.

Indra, the king of the heavens, granted Kunti a son named **Arjuna**. He was born with long and mighty arms to wield the bow and sharp reflexes to win battles.

Madri was gifted twin sons, **Nakula** and **Sahadeva**, by the Ashwini Kumaras, the twin gods of healing. Both boys shone with divine radiance and were handsome and intelligent.

The five brothers grew up in the forest. They were inseparable, and each was ready to sacrifice his life for the other.

Sadly, both Pandu and Madri died when the Pandavas were but children.

It was after this that they were taken by their widowed mother, Kunti, to live in the palace of Hastinapur.

In Pandu's absence, Dhritarashtra was ruling Hastinapur under the guidance of his uncle Bheeshma and his half-brother, the wise Vidura.

His dislike for the dead Pandu was replaced by a growing hatred for the Pandavas.

He especially resented the fact that the eldest Pandava, Yudhishthira, was older than his son Duryodhana. This made Yudhishthira the first choice for the crown prince of Hastinapur.

However, Dhritarashtra never spoke his sentiments aloud.

The Pandavas, with their kindness and honesty, naturally attracted the affection of their elders.

Bheeshma would spend long hours telling them stories of their ancestors.

Vidura often praised them loudly, declaring that they would bring fame to the Kuru throne.

But all this while...

...it was envy that grew in Duryodhana's jealous heart. He could not bear to see his poor cousins from the forest receive the goodwill of the elders.

Under his direction, the hundred Kaurava brothers took every opportunity to pick unfair quarrels with the Pandavas.

THWACK!

Though they were five pitted against a hundred, the Pandavas always fought back. With their divine strength, they overpowered the Kauravas each time.

GLUGG

This only served to anger the Kauravas even more.

Days passed, and the Pandavas and Kauravas started taking formal instruction in the art of warfare and weaponry under Dronacharya. Though born a Brahmin, member of a class known for their knowledge of the scriptures, Drona was also a formidable warrior.

Through years of training, the one hundred and five princes grew to become skilled Kshatriyas. The Kauravas were deadly warriors, but the Pandavas naturally excelled.

Drona marvelled at the grace of the five boys. Yudhishthira favoured the javelin, Bheema the mace, while the twins were expert swordsmen.

But it was Arjuna who was Drona's favourite. He shone as a brilliant archer. None could match Arjuna's skills – not even Drona's own son, Ashwatthama.

Ashwatthama watched Arjuna with envy, and this did not go unnoticed by Duryodhana.

Ashwatthama and Duryodhana became comrades, joined in their hatred for the Pandavas.

Soon the time came when the princes were of age, ready to take up the mantle of ruling the kingdom.

Yudhishthira was heir to the throne, but neither Dhritarashtra nor Duryodhana acknowledged this truth.

Blind with greed, Dhritarashtra was reluctant to give up his power, and with his son's coaxing, delayed passing the throne to the heir.

And so it came to pass that in his desire to become king, Duryodhana began to plot the murder of his cousins.

Duryodhana found a loyal friend and a fellow conspirator in the mighty **Karna**, the adopted son of a humble charioteer. He was a warrior with uncanny abilities and superior skills that exceeded even those of the Pandavas.

Despite his prowess, Karna did not receive his due respect from Kshatriyas. He was considered 'low born' since he was the son of a mere charioteer.

However, Karna wore a gold armour and earrings that were attached to his skin since his birth. These hinted at his mysterious celestial origin, but most of us were blind to it, until the very end.

Duryodhana recognised Karna's abilities and bestowed his favour upon him by crowning him king of Anga, a small province.

Karna was overwhelmed by Duryodhana's favour and would remain loyal to the Kauravas till his last breath.

On the other hand, the Pandavas formed a lasting friendship with their maternal cousin **Krishna,** a prince of the Yadava clan. Kunti was Krishna's aunt.

But long before I entered the lives of the Pandavas, Krishna had already entered mine...

Krishna! How can I describe him? Words are not enough to do justice to that mischievous, magnificent being!

It was as if he could read my mind. When I was sad, Krishna would arrive, and the sound of his flute would soon fill the air.

His joyful, yet serene presence always made my heart happy.

Krishna, a trusted friend of my father, was the only man who respected my intelligence enough to spar with me as an equal.

We would discuss philosophy and politics for hours.

Krishna would often speak to me of his cousins, the Pandavas, and from him I learnt all about them.

He often hinted at my troubled future, but I was too confident of my life to take him seriously. While I would jest, he would look me in the eye...

Much will be asked of you in the years to come. But remember that you are born with the strength to give it.

As long as you promise to make me laugh, Krishna, I am content with anything that comes my way.

You, content? Why, that sounds impossible!

HAHAHA!

How true his words were! How naive I was about myself and my life!

Of the Pandavas, Arjuna and Krishna eventually became best friends and spent much of their time together.

As children of gods themselves, the Pandavas realised that Krishna was actually the human incarnation of Lord Vishnu*. So they looked to Krishna for guidance...

...for ensnared in Duryodhana's evil plans, the Pandavas needed all the help they could get.

*One of the divine trinity in the Hindu pantheon. Also known as the Great Preserver.

Duryodhana secretly built a palace made of lacquer in a city called Varanavata, and persuaded the Pandavas and Kunti to spend some time in its luxury.

When the Pandavas were resting in the palace at night, Duryodhana ordered it to be set on fire.

But luck was on the Pandavas' side, and with Vidura's assistance, they narrowly escaped from the burning palace.

It was after this that my destiny was linked with the Pandavas. My wedding was unusual, and like none other held before. I was married to all five brothers, but...

...this is not the moment to speak of my wedding. Let me continue with the story of the Pandavas for now.

When the Pandavas felt safe enough to reveal themselves to Duryodhana, he was surprised and disappointed to see his cousins alive and well.

Since Dhritarashtra was reluctant to hand over the kingdom to Yudhishthira, Bheeshma and Vidura urged him to divide the kingdom so that the Pandavas and the Kauravas could live in peace. The miserly Dhritarashtra gifted the Pandavas the barren half of his land.

It was a wasteland called **Khandavaprastha**.

The Pandavas realised they had been given a bad deal. Nevertheless, Yudhishthira accepted Khandavaprastha with gratitude, out of respect for his uncle...

...and Dhritarashtra crowned Yudhishthira king of Khandavaprastha.

Yudhishthira now turned to Krishna for guidance in establishing the new kingdom. Krishna invoked the presence of Indra, king of the heavens.

With Indra's blessings and under the care of the divine architect, Vishwakarma, the wasteland of Khandavaprastha was transformed into a city of wonders.

It became famous for its beauty and splendour. Its palaces shone, and its streets were wide and clean.

Its lands were now rich and fertile, yielding food in plenty. Its citizens were happy under the benevolent rule of Yudhishthira and his four brothers.

People from far and wide visited the city of the Pandavas to witness its grandeur. It was almost as magnificent as the realms of Indra and the gods.

After this miraculous change, Khandavaprastha was given a new name – **Indraprastha**.

With his just and wise rule, the prowess of his brothers, and the benign guidance of Krishna, Yudhishthira gained the support of all the kingdoms in Bhaaratvarsha. So, he performed the fire ritual of the *rajasuya yajna* and became the king of kings.

Indraprastha celebrated for weeks. The city overflowed with royal guests, and the Pandavas honoured each one of them. Kings and queens, revered sages, and even common folk travelled to the kingdom to witness this event. The air echoed with their praise for Yudhishthira.

The breathtaking majesty of Indraprastha was revealed to Duryodhana and the other Kauravas. They gaped in wonder at the bejewelled walls of the palace, the verdant fields, and the bustling life of the city. How had the Pandavas transformed a wasteland into this?

The fire of hatred had been burning too long for Duryodhana. The grandeur of Indraprastha was too much for his jealous heart to bear.

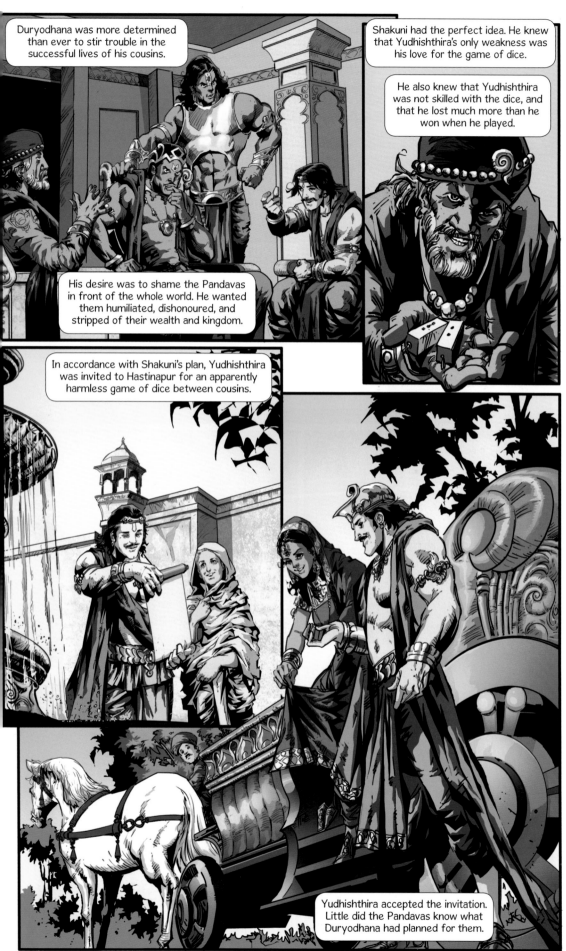

Duryodhana was more determined than ever to stir trouble in the successful lives of his cousins.

Shakuni had the perfect idea. He knew that Yudhishthira's only weakness was his love for the game of dice.

He also knew that Yudhishthira was not skilled with the dice, and that he lost much more than he won when he played.

His desire was to shame the Pandavas in front of the whole world. He wanted them humiliated, dishonoured, and stripped of their wealth and kingdom.

In accordance with Shakuni's plan, Yudhishthira was invited to Hastinapur for an apparently harmless game of dice between cousins.

Yudhishthira accepted the invitation. Little did the Pandavas know what Duryodhana had planned for them.

The game began in earnest. In the royal court of Hastinapur, under the blind gaze of Dhritarashtra, sly Shakuni rolled the dice on behalf of Duryodhana.

With his poor skills, Yudhishthira was no match for Shakuni and his tainted dice.

To begin with, Yudhishthira wagered his ornaments and wealth...

...then his servants...

...and then his kingdom, Indraprastha...

...and lost them all to Duryodhana in quick succession.

But the fever of the game fired Yudhishthira's blood. On Shakuni's provocation, he wagered his twin brothers Nakula and Sahadeva...

...and lost them.

With his cunning words, Shakuni goaded Yudhishthira into staking his brothers Bheema and Arjuna, and finally, even himself.

He lost all three wagers.

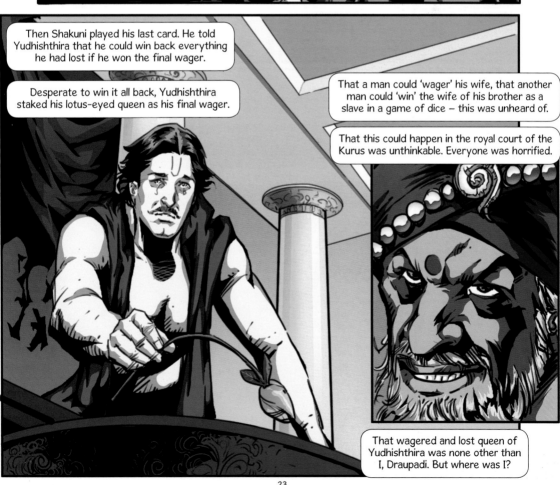

Then Shakuni played his last card. He told Yudhishthira that he could win back everything he had lost if he won the final wager.

Desperate to win it all back, Yudhishthira staked his lotus-eyed queen as his final wager.

That a man could 'wager' his wife, that another man could 'win' the wife of his brother as a slave in a game of dice – this was unheard of.

That this could happen in the royal court of the Kurus was unthinkable. Everyone was horrified.

That wagered and lost queen of Yudhishthira was none other than I, Draupadi. But where was I?

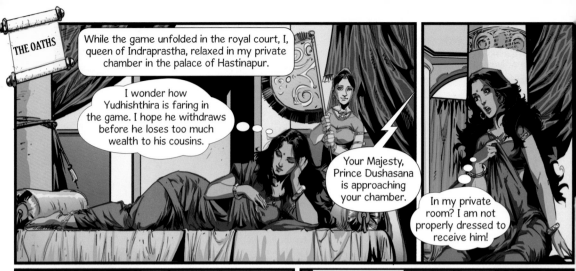

While the game unfolded in the royal court, I, queen of Indraprastha, relaxed in my private chamber in the palace of Hastinapur.

I wonder how Yudhishthira is faring in the game. I hope he withdraws before he loses too much wealth to his cousins.

Your Majesty, Prince Dushasana is approaching your chamber.

In my private room? I am not properly dressed to receive him!

There you are, servant woman! You have been summoned to the court by your new master.

How dare you call me a servant woman? I am the queen of Indraprastha!

HAHAHAHA! Queen! Not any more! Your husband has lost everything in the game of dice – his kingdom, his brothers, himself, and even you.

Oh Yudhishthira!

As a servant of the Kauravas you must now obey our command. Come with me to the court, or I will drag you there. **Now!**

This cannot be happening! Dear gods!

Queen Gandhari! If I make it to her chamber she will protect me from her sons' madness.

Stop!

AAAAAHHHHH!

You think you can escape your destiny?

Pain ripped through my body and my soul! I was dragged through the palace like an animal and flung on the floor of the court.

What have I done to deserve this?

Here she is. Our new slave.

Bheeshma, Dronacharya, and Vidura hung their heads in shame.

Is Draupadi here, Vidura?

She is... my lord... this is such a dark day in our lives!

Bound by the rules of the game, the Pandavas helplessly watched through a curtain of tears as I begged for justice from the elders of the court.

Dushasana!!

Great-uncle Bheeshma! I have been dragged here in a state of undress. I have been thrown to the floor and called a slave!

No woman deserves such degrading treatment! Please have me escorted back to my chamber!

But my plea fell on deaf ears. Though he was devastated by this turn of events, Bheeshma did not rise to help me. My voice turned cold with anger.

My father would never have dreamt that the illustrious Kuru clan could shame his daughter in public. I demand respect from this court!

Since the members of this court seem to have forgotten, let me remind them of the story of my birth...

It was several years ago that the Kauravas and my husbands, the five Pandava princes, had successfully completed their training under Dronacharya.

I have given you all the knowledge I have. You are ready, my disciples. Be the fearless warriors you were born to be!

Guru Drona, we are indebted to you. Please tell me what you desire as *gurudakshina**. We shall search the heavens, if we must, and bring it to you.

*Fee or gift given to a guru by his student after successfully completing the training

Dronacharya had waited for years for exactly this moment.

As my dakshina, I want all of you to capture Drupada, the king of Panchala. Bring him to me alive.

Is that all? You shall have him.

Do not underestimate Drupada. He is a brilliant warrior.

Fear not, Guru Drona. You have taught us well.

The Kauravas refused to join forces with the Pandavas, so both went separately on the same mission.

26

My father, King Drupada, and his army rode out to meet the challenge of the Kuru princes. The Kauravas were soon defeated.

When the Pandavas advanced, King Drupada was surprised at the impertinence of the young princes. Did they not know his might as a warrior?

Young fools! They come without an army. They will meet their death in minutes!

He had never been proved so wrong! Within moments, the Pandavas cleared a path through the Panchala army to his chariot.

What incredible archery! This prince is a lion among warriors! My heart is glad to see a man with such skills!

Then Arjuna let loose thousands of arrows that formed a shield around my father's chariot.

Under the haze of Arjuna's arrows, the Pandavas grabbed Drupada from his chariot, bound him as a prisoner, and left the battlefield taking the beleaguered king along with them.

Without its king, the Panchala army gave up the fight.

Guru Drona, here is King Drupada of Panchala.

You have done well, Pandavas.

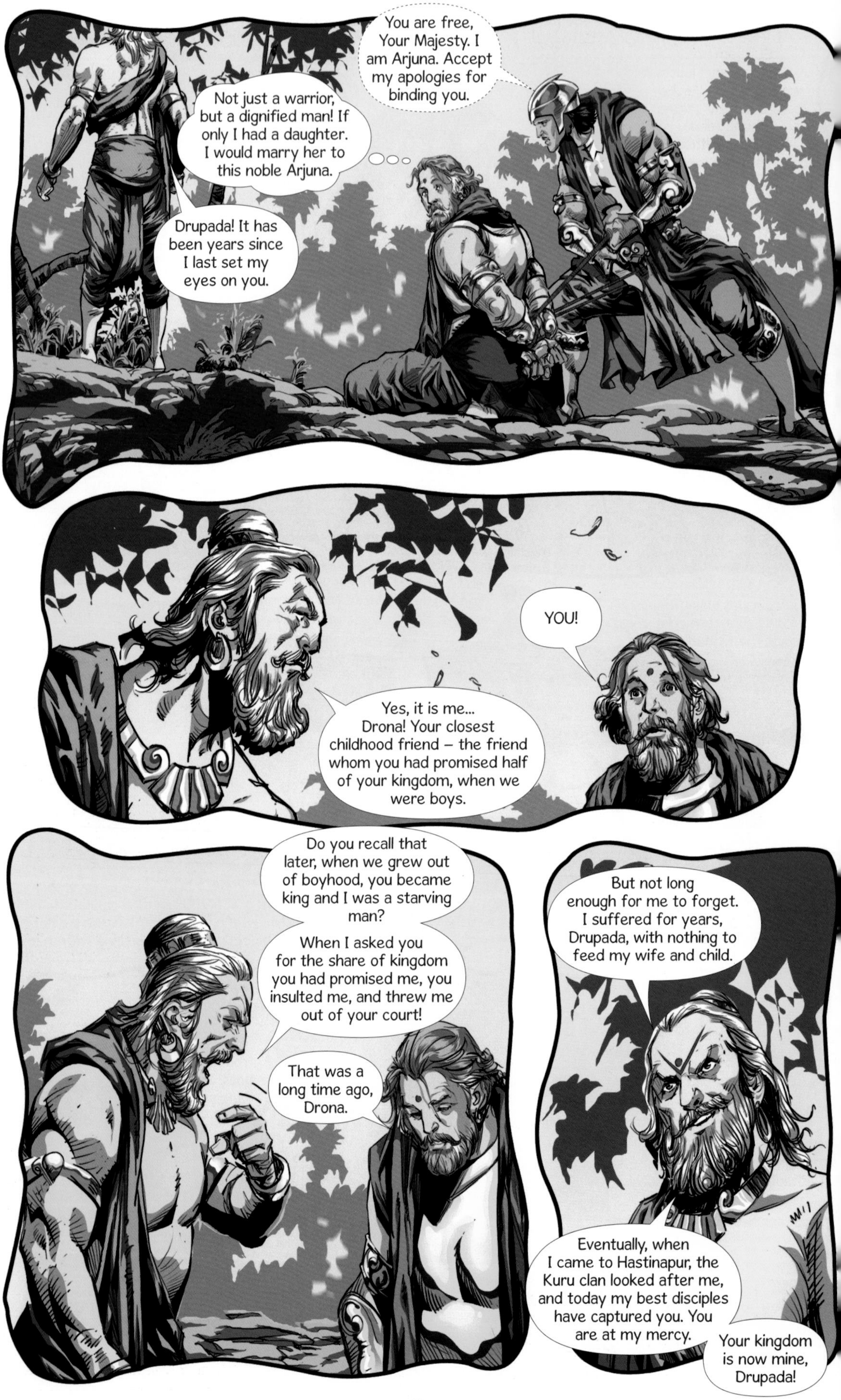
Drupada! It has been years since I last set my eyes on you.
Not just a warrior, but a dignified man! If only I had a daughter. I would marry her to this noble Arjuna.
You are free, Your Majesty. I am Arjuna. Accept my apologies for binding you.
YOU!
Yes, it is me... Drona! Your closest childhood friend – the friend whom you had promised half of your kingdom, when we were boys.
Do you recall that later, when we grew out of boyhood, you became king and I was a starving man?
When I asked you for the share of kingdom you had promised me, you insulted me, and threw me out of your court!
That was a long time ago, Drona.
But not long enough for me to forget. I suffered for years, Drupada, with nothing to feed my wife and child.
Eventually, when I came to Hastinapur, the Kuru clan looked after me, and today my best disciples have captured you. You are at my mercy.
Your kingdom is now mine, Drupada!

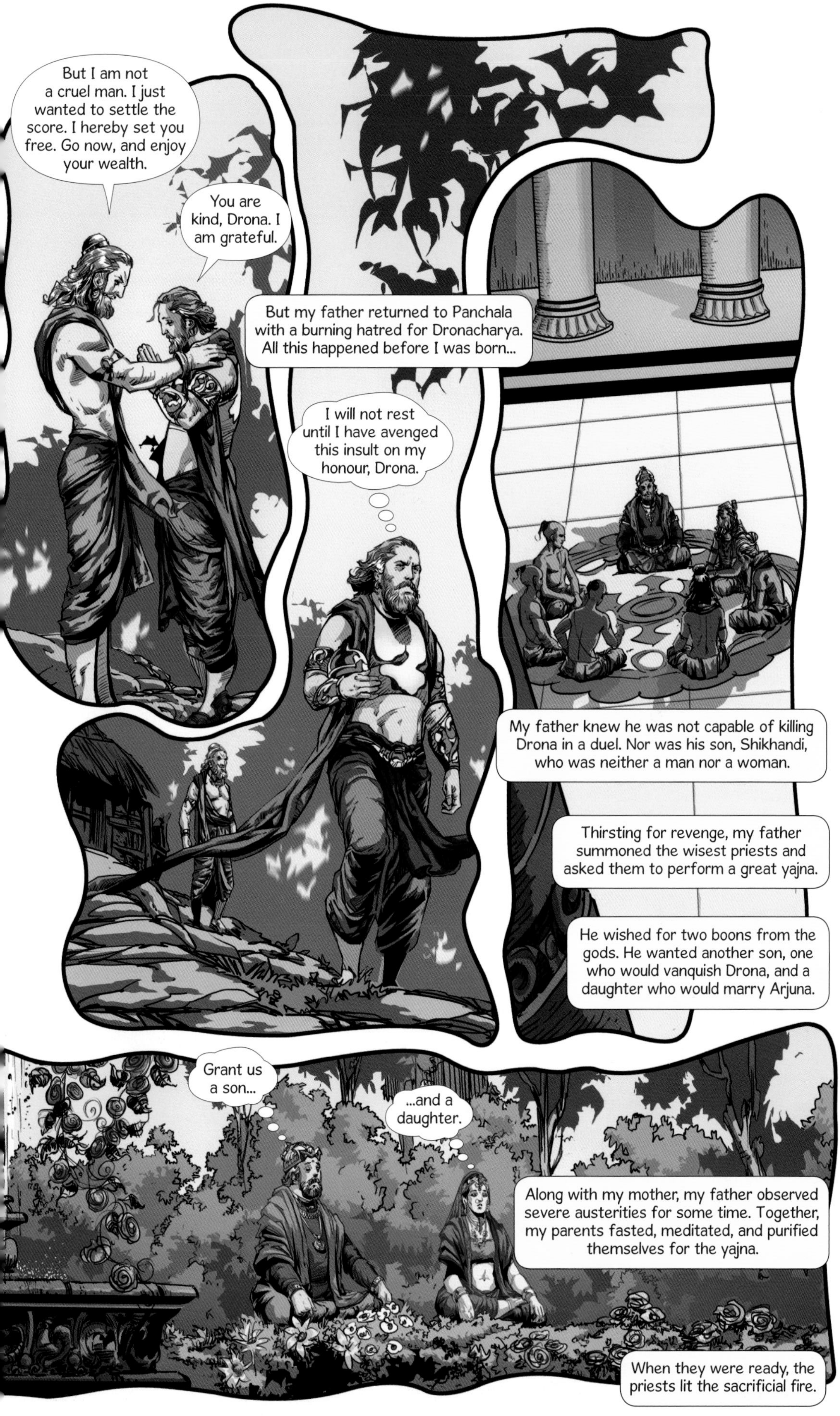

But I am not a cruel man. I just wanted to settle the score. I hereby set you free. Go now, and enjoy your wealth.
You are kind, Drona. I am grateful.
But my father returned to Panchala with a burning hatred for Dronacharya. All this happened before I was born...
I will not rest until I have avenged this insult on my honour, Drona.
My father knew he was not capable of killing Drona in a duel. Nor was his son, Shikhandi, who was neither a man nor a woman.
Thirsting for revenge, my father summoned the wisest priests and asked them to perform a great yajna.
He wished for two boons from the gods. He wanted another son, one who would vanquish Drona, and a daughter who would marry Arjuna.
Grant us a son...
...and a daughter.
Along with my mother, my father observed severe austerities for some time. Together, my parents fasted, meditated, and purified themselves for the yajna.
When they were ready, the priests lit the sacrificial fire.

Sacred hymns were chanted. Oblations were made. As flames leapt up to the sky, my parents sat with bated breath, waiting for their prayers to be answered.

Then, a god-like young man arose from the flames. He was sheathed in golden armour and carried his divine weapons with him. His eyes blazed amber, the colour of fire, and there was no doubt that he was a supreme warrior. A prophecy resounded in the skies as he appeared.

This youth shall be known as **Dhrishtadyumna.** He is a gift from the gods to Drupada!

Dhrishtadyumna is born to kill Drona!

O king of Panchala, what you desire, arises from the sacred fire. Here is your son.

Thus, my father was granted his first wish. But there was more to come.

The priests poured more offerings into the fire, and from its orange heat, they watched a maiden arise.

Dark-complexioned and dark-eyed, and with hair fragrant as the blue lotus, I stood before my parents. The heavens shook. Thunder rumbled across the sky as a prophecy echoed...

Lotus-eyed and bewitching, this maiden is the best of women. Her beauty is unmatched on heaven and earth. Her dusky skin gives her the name **Krishnaa**.

As the princess of Panchala, she will be called **Panchali**. And as the daughter of Drupada, she will be known as **Draupadi**.

This woman will be the cause of the destruction of all evil Kshatriyas. That is the divine purpose of her birth.

This maiden is created from the beauty of the goddess Shree herself. To fulfil your second wish, O King, here is your daughter.

At last! I have a lovely daughter who will be the perfect wife to the handsome Arjuna.

Thus, I was born... not from a mother's womb, but from the flaming arms of Fire as a grown woman...

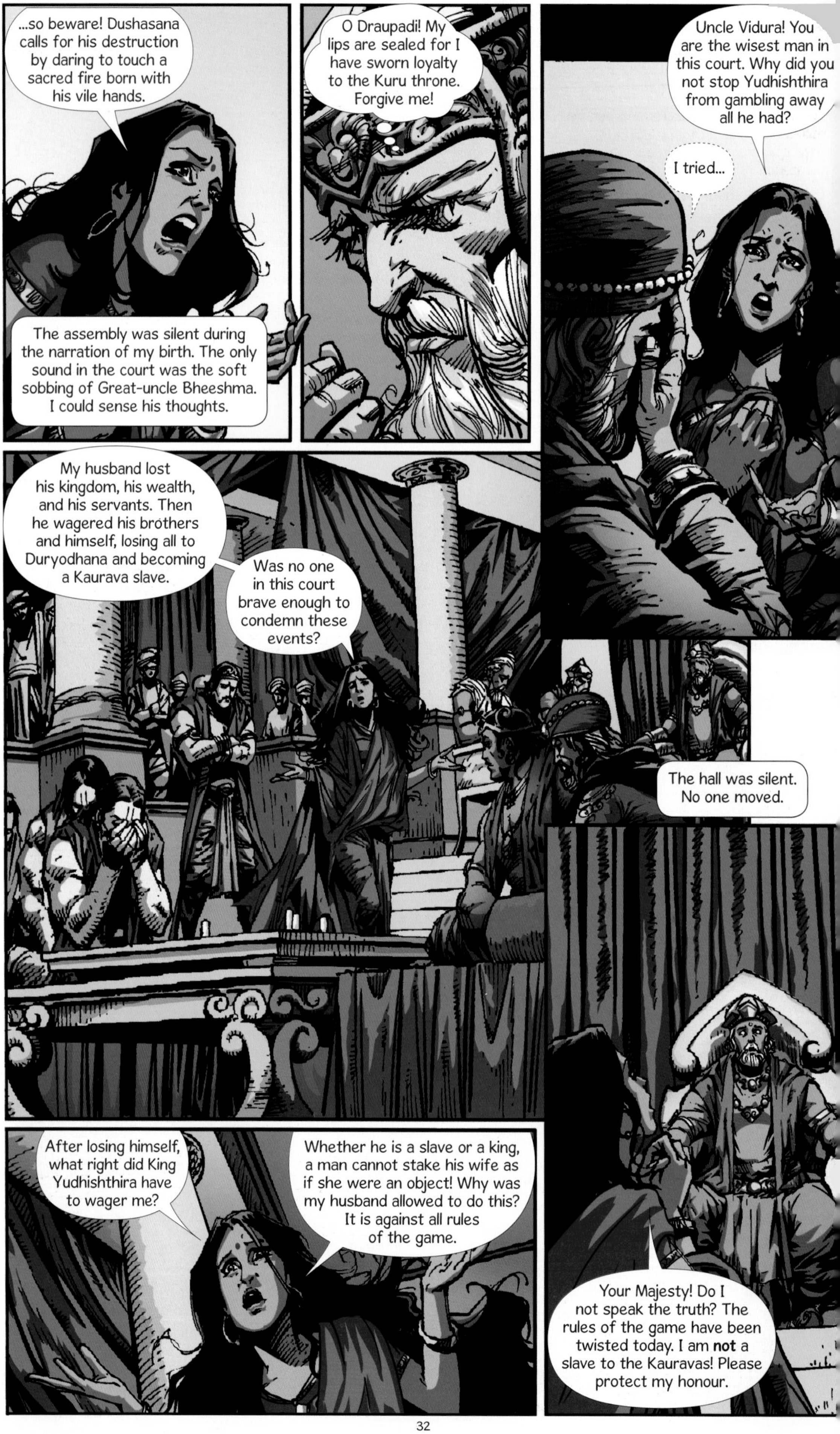
...so beware! Dushasana calls for his destruction by daring to touch a sacred fire born with his vile hands.
The assembly was silent during the narration of my birth. The only sound in the court was the soft sobbing of Great-uncle Bheeshma. I could sense his thoughts.
O Draupadi! My lips are sealed for I have sworn loyalty to the Kuru throne. Forgive me!
Uncle Vidura! You are the wisest man in this court. Why did you not stop Yudhishthira from gambling away all he had?
I tried...
My husband lost his kingdom, his wealth, and his servants. Then he wagered his brothers and himself, losing all to Duryodhana and becoming a Kaurava slave.
Was no one in this court brave enough to condemn these events?
The hall was silent. No one moved.
After losing himself, what right did King Yudhishthira have to wager me?
Whether he is a slave or a king, a man cannot stake his wife as if she were an object! Why was my husband allowed to do this? It is against all rules of the game.
Your Majesty! Do I not speak the truth? The rules of the game have been twisted today. I am **not** a slave to the Kauravas! Please protect my honour.

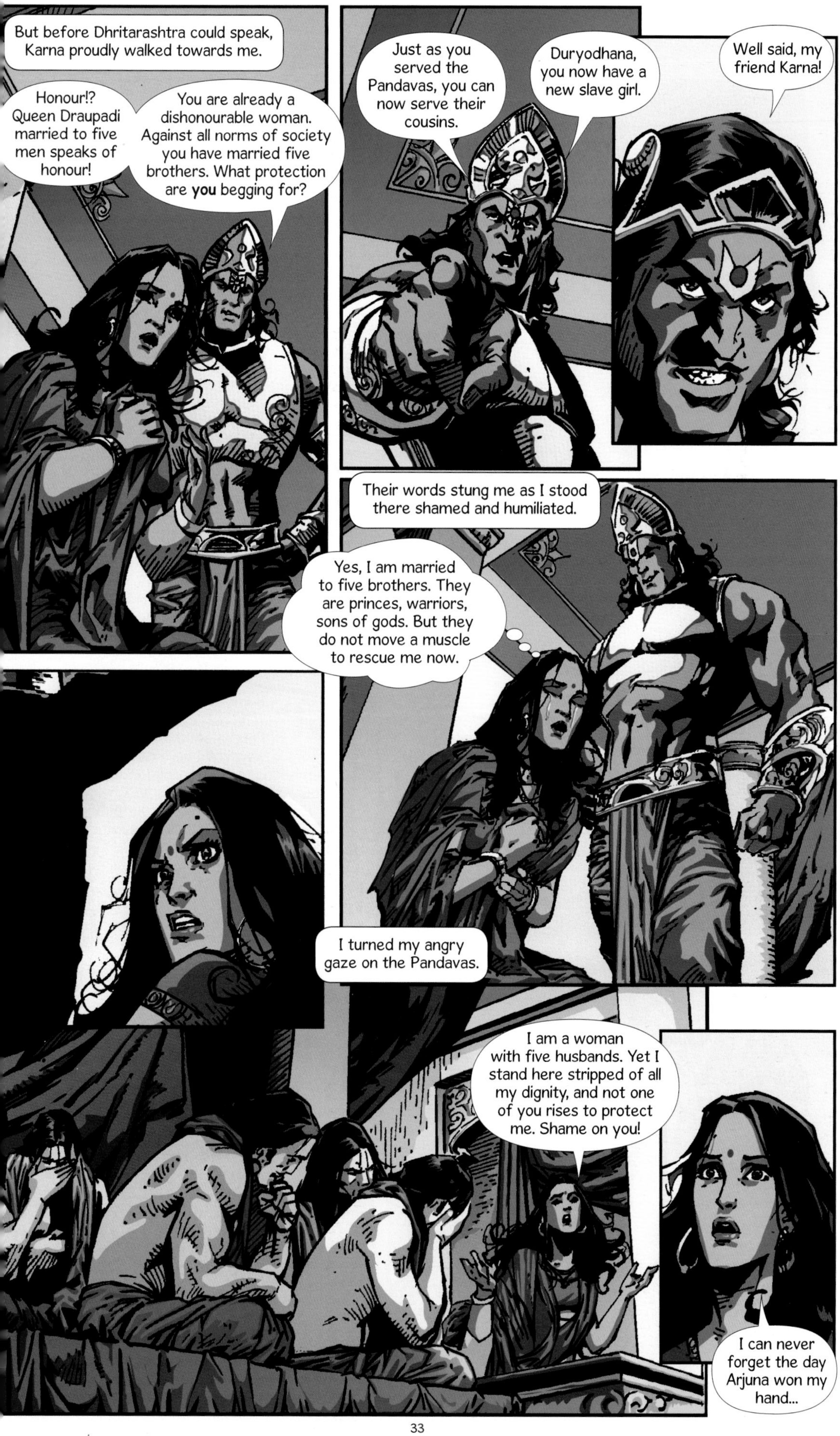
But before Dhritarashtra could speak, Karna proudly walked towards me.
Honour!? Queen Draupadi married to five men speaks of honour!
You are already a dishonourable woman. Against all norms of society you have married five brothers. What protection are **you** begging for?
Just as you served the Pandavas, you can now serve their cousins.
Duryodhana, you now have a new slave girl.
Well said, my friend Karna!
Their words stung me as I stood there shamed and humiliated.
Yes, I am married to five brothers. They are princes, warriors, sons of gods. But they do not move a muscle to rescue me now.
I turned my angry gaze on the Pandavas.
I am a woman with five husbands. Yet I stand here stripped of all my dignity, and not one of you rises to protect me. Shame on you!
I can never forget the day Arjuna won my hand...

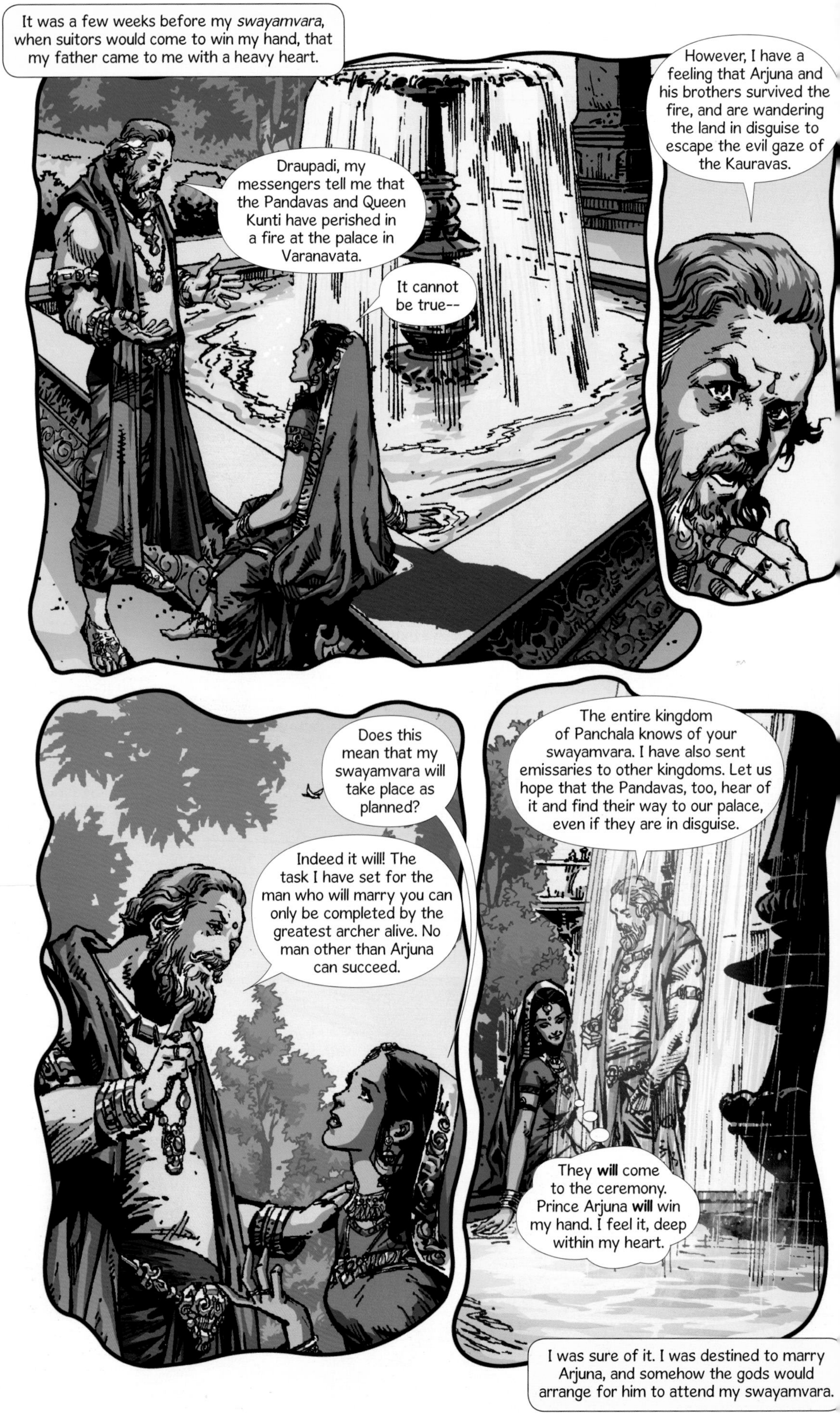
It was a few weeks before my *swayamvara*, when suitors would come to win my hand, that my father came to me with a heavy heart.
Draupadi, my messengers tell me that the Pandavas and Queen Kunti have perished in a fire at the palace in Varanavata.
It cannot be true--
However, I have a feeling that Arjuna and his brothers survived the fire, and are wandering the land in disguise to escape the evil gaze of the Kauravas.
Does this mean that my swayamvara will take place as planned?
Indeed it will! The task I have set for the man who will marry you can only be completed by the greatest archer alive. No man other than Arjuna can succeed.
The entire kingdom of Panchala knows of your swayamvara. I have also sent emissaries to other kingdoms. Let us hope that the Pandavas, too, hear of it and find their way to our palace, even if they are in disguise.
They **will** come to the ceremony. Prince Arjuna **will** win my hand. I feel it, deep within my heart.
I was sure of it. I was destined to marry Arjuna, and somehow the gods would arrange for him to attend my swayamvara.

Finally, the day arrived. There was much excitement and anticipation in the palace, which was beautifully decorated for the occasion.

Dressed in bridal finery, I greeted my dearest friend, Krishna.

Krishna! Bless me so I may find happiness!

Though it sounds unlikely, fate will present you with a choice today. Two great archers and two different destinies. Choose well, Panchali.

My brother, Dhrishtadyumna, spoke to the assembled guests and explained to them the task.

Respected kings and princes! To win my sister's hand, this mighty bow must be lifted and strung.

The contestant must then hit the rotating fish in the eye with five arrows, by merely looking at its reflection in the water below.

Whosoever will accomplish this task successfully shall win the hand of my sister in marriage.

Several princes and kings tried their hand at the task. But they all failed miserably. Even Duryodhana and Dushasana could not hit the target.

Then Karna rose. Shining like the sun, he lifted the bow with the practised ease of a superior marksman. I was amazed. So this was the second great archer Krishna spoke of!

Krishna's advice to choose well echoed in my ears.

No one could equal Arjuna's skill as an archer, but Karna. I had been born to marry Arjuna, and my destiny, pulsing in my blood, made me spit out cruel words.

Karna returned to his seat, bitter and angry. And I regretted my insulting words. But I had not seen any other way of choosing Arjuna over him.

Stop!

I will not marry the low-born son of a charioteer. I am a princess, and I will marry a Kshatriya or a Brahmin. These are my conditions.

None of the Kshatriyas present have completed the task, Father!

Patience, my son. There might be a Brahmin in this gathering who is well-versed in the art of archery.

My eyes lit up as a handsome Brahmin youth strode to the centre of the arena.

He calmly strung the bow, gazed at the reflection of the moving fish...

...and hit the target with five arrows. The spectators were awed by this feat of archery. My heart thudded with excitement.

Before anyone could protest, I walked up to the Brahmin. I looked at his powerful shoulders, and the ease with which he held the bow.

His eyes reminded me of Krishna's.

Besides Karna, only Arjuna could have succeeded at this feat. You must be Arjuna the brave.

But the Kshatriyas gathered in the arena were not pleased to be outwitted by a Brahmin.

Jayadratha, Shalya, Shakuni, Duryodhana, and many others drew their weapons, eager to slay my chosen husband and his four Brahmin brothers.

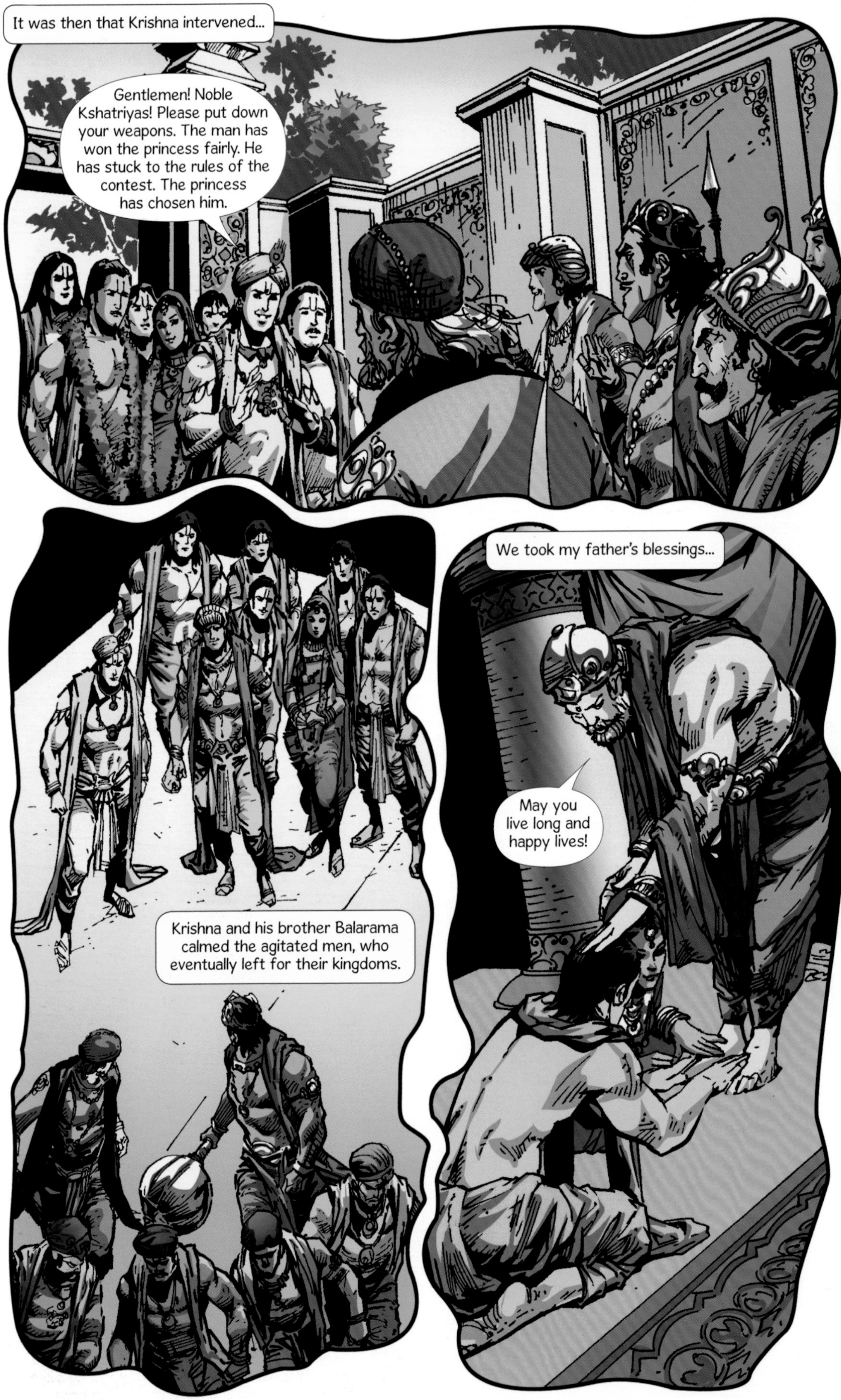
It was then that Krishna intervened...
Gentlemen! Noble Kshatriyas! Please put down your weapons. The man has won the princess fairly. He has stuck to the rules of the contest. The princess has chosen him.
Krishna and his brother Balarama calmed the agitated men, who eventually left for their kingdoms.
We took my father's blessings...
May you live long and happy lives!

...and then my husband led me out of the royal grounds. Along with us walked his four brothers. All five men had the fearless gait of lions and the radiance of gods. Though I had been confident of my husband's identity, any last dregs of doubt were cleared when the brothers spoke.

Yudhishthira! Arjuna! Nakula! So these are the Pandavas! I was right.

Arjuna! You were so fast and accurate with those arrows!

Well done, Arjuna! We are all proud of you.

Thank you, Yudhishthira! Thank you, Nakula!

We were approaching a humble cottage when the twin brothers ran ahead to its doorstep.

Mother! Look what we have brought home today!

In the cottage sat Queen Kunti, disguised in simple clothes. Busy with the preparation of food, she did not look up from her work.

Whatever you have brought, share it equally amongst the five of you, my sons!

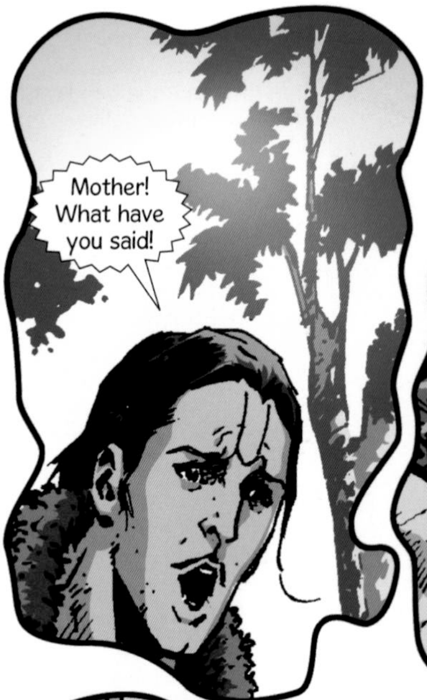
Mother! What have you said!

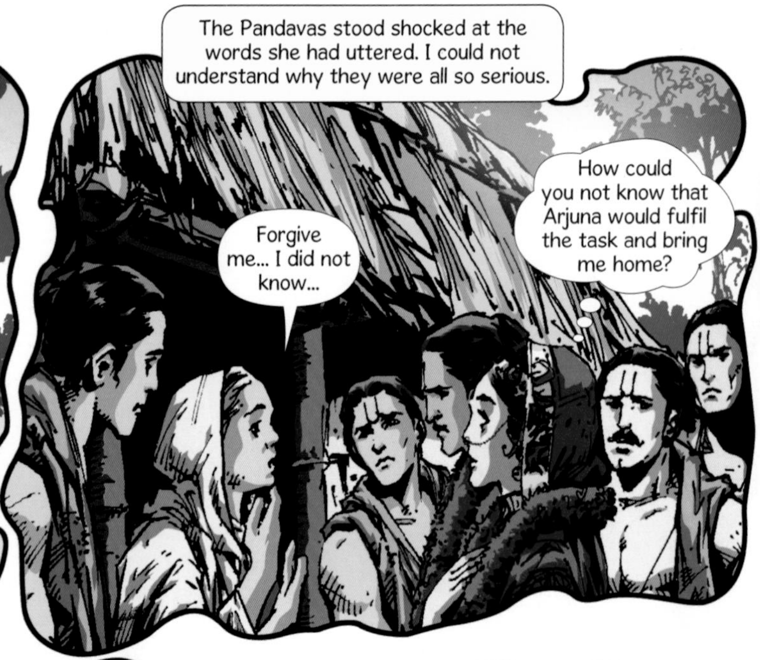
The Pandavas stood shocked at the words she had uttered. I could not understand why they were all so serious.
Forgive me... I did not know...
How could you not know that Arjuna would fulfil the task and bring me home?

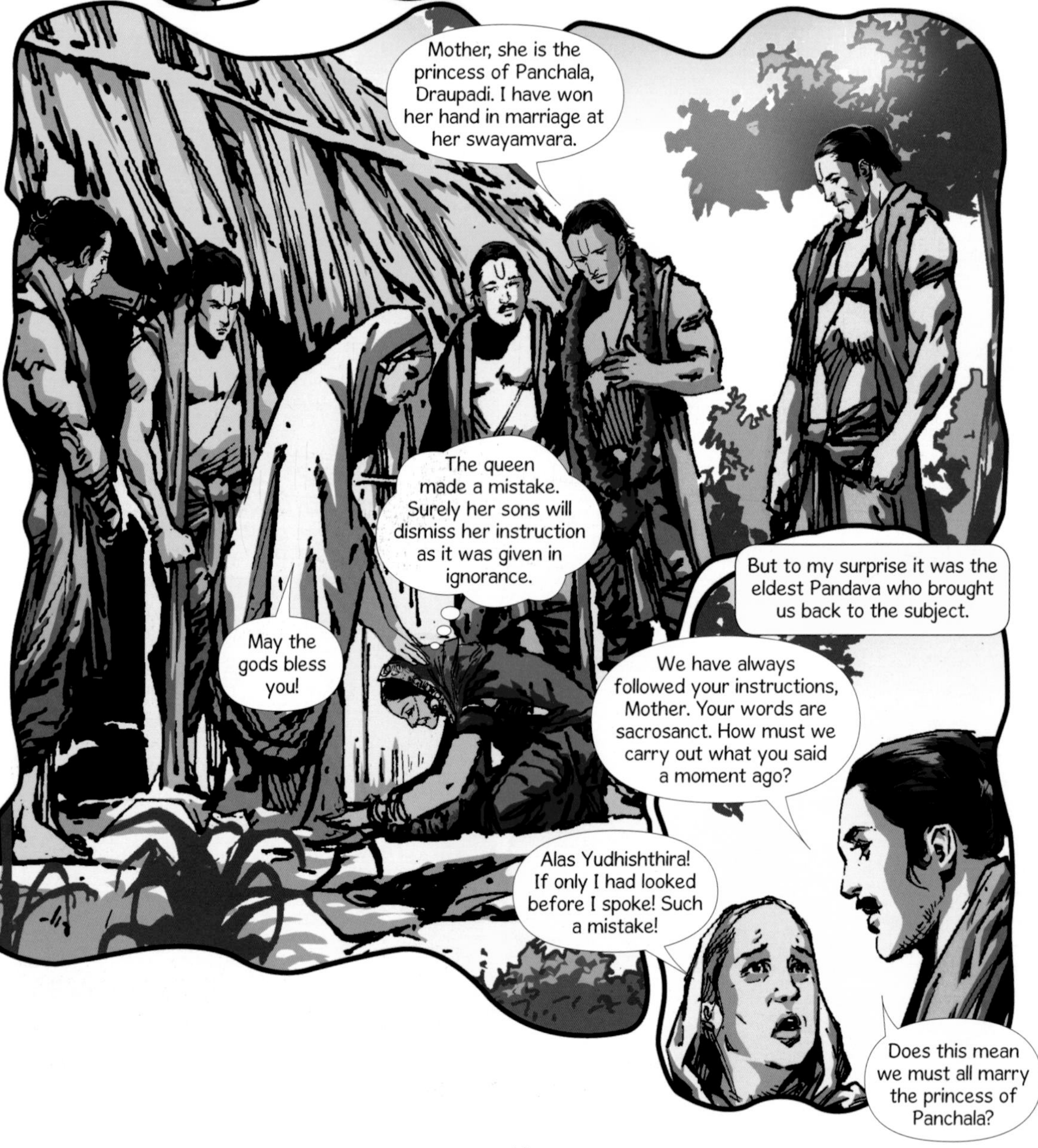
Mother, she is the princess of Panchala, Draupadi. I have won her hand in marriage at her swayamvara.
The queen made a mistake. Surely her sons will dismiss her instruction as it was given in ignorance.
May the gods bless you!
But to my surprise it was the eldest Pandava who brought us back to the subject.
We have always followed your instructions, Mother. Your words are sacrosanct. How must we carry out what you said a moment ago?
Alas Yudhishthira! If only I had looked before I spoke! Such a mistake!
Does this mean we must all marry the princess of Panchala?

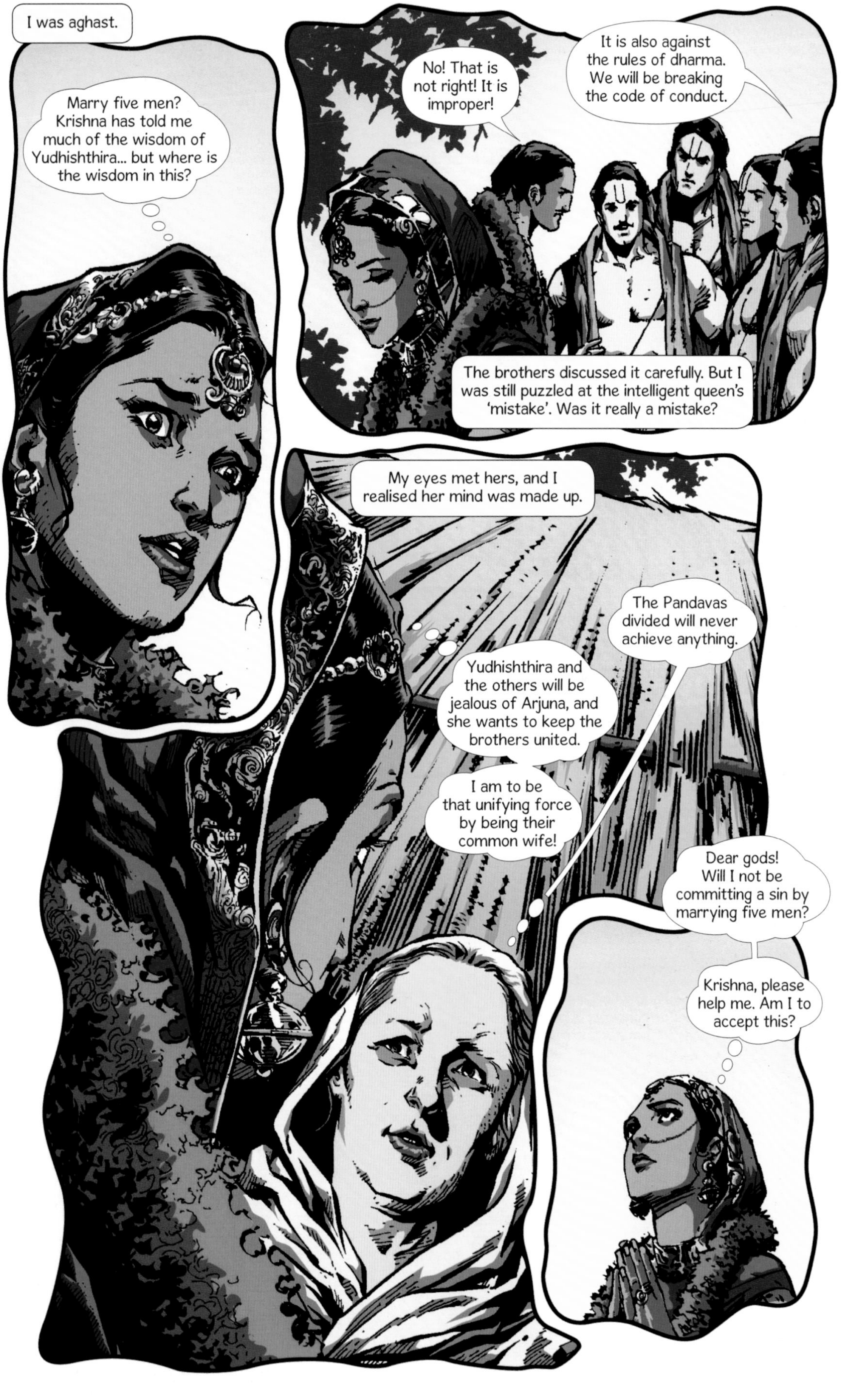
I was aghast.
Marry five men? Krishna has told me much of the wisdom of Yudhishthira... but where is the wisdom in this?
No! That is not right! It is improper!
It is also against the rules of dharma. We will be breaking the code of conduct.
The brothers discussed it carefully. But I was still puzzled at the intelligent queen's 'mistake'. Was it really a mistake?
My eyes met hers, and I realised her mind was made up.
The Pandavas divided will never achieve anything.
Yudhishthira and the others will be jealous of Arjuna, and she wants to keep the brothers united.
I am to be that unifying force by being their common wife!
Dear gods! Will I not be committing a sin by marrying five men?
Krishna, please help me. Am I to accept this?

My mind was buffeted by winds of uncertainty, when Maharishi Vyasa arrived accompanied by my father and brother.

With my divine vision, I saw your difficult situation.

The remedy is obvious — Draupadi must marry all five brothers. But first, I must put to rest all your doubts.

Princess, in your last incarnation, you were a young girl who performed severe austerities. Pleased with your penance, Lord Shiva* appeared before you...

*One of the divine trinity in the Hindu pantheon. Also known as the Great Destroyer.

Ask what you wish for!

Lord, please grant me a handsome husband... a husband who lives by the codes of conduct... a husband with supernatural strength... a peerless warrior... and a wise and gentle man.

You have asked for a husband with five different qualities. But in your next life, you will incarnate in an age when all these qualities would be impossible to find in one man.

Therefore, you will marry five heroic men in your next life — each possessing one of the five qualities you desire.

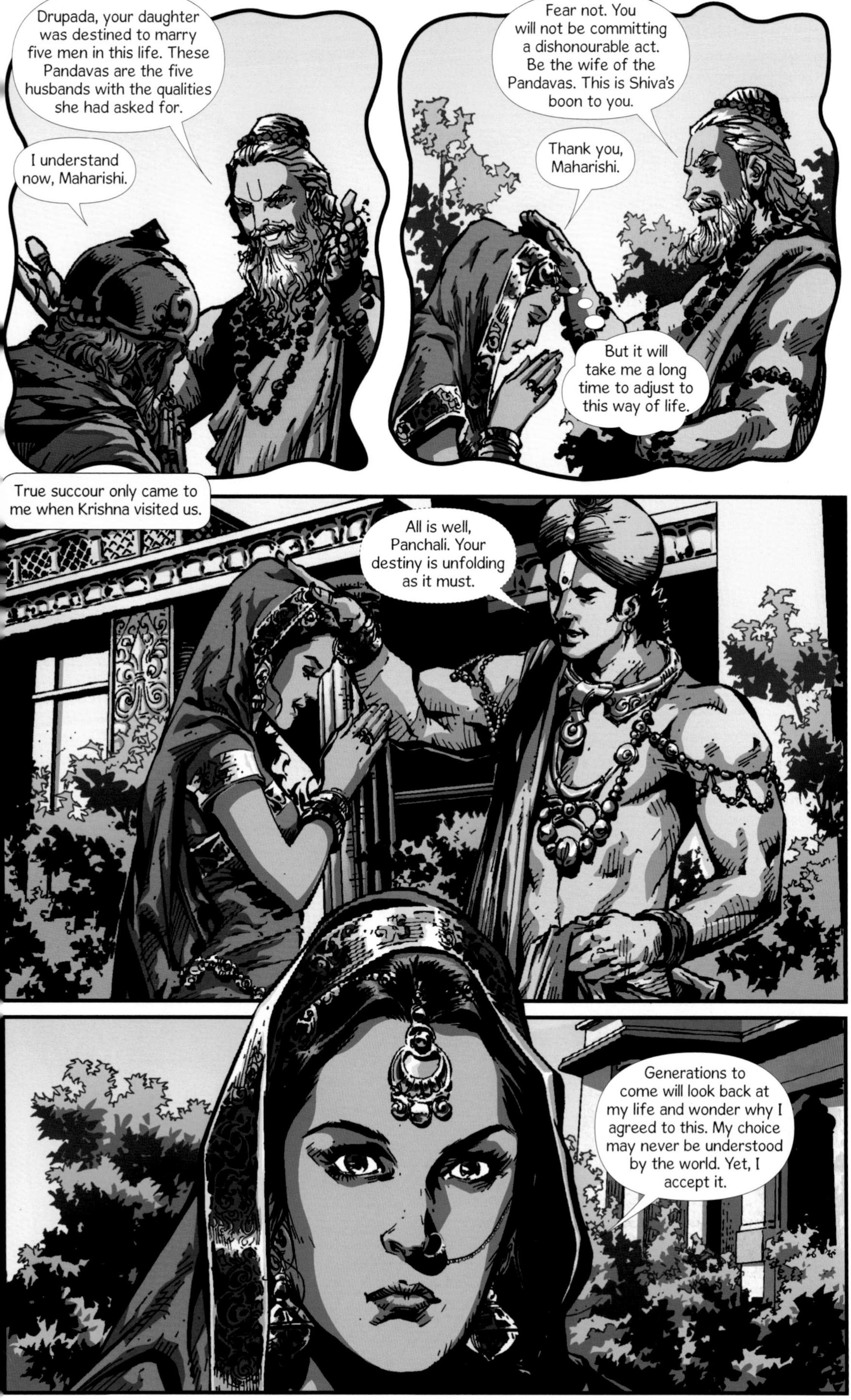
Drupada, your daughter was destined to marry five men in this life. These Pandavas are the five husbands with the qualities she had asked for.
I understand now, Maharishi.
Fear not. You will not be committing a dishonourable act. Be the wife of the Pandavas. This is Shiva's boon to you.
Thank you, Maharishi.
But it will take me a long time to adjust to this way of life.
True succour only came to me when Krishna visited us.
All is well, Panchali. Your destiny is unfolding as it must.
Generations to come will look back at my life and wonder why I agreed to this. My choice may never be understood by the world. Yet, I accept it.

With the blessings of Maharishi Vyasa, there were five wedding ceremonies, and I was married to each Pandava.

I reminded myself that I was fortunate to be wedded to such noble men who were gentle and respectful.

Krishna was present at the weddings and continued to reassure us that we were taking the right step. He showered us with gifts and gave us his unconditional support.

Queen Kunti was happy to see her sons united. I was confident, that married to these valiant princes, no harm could ever come to me.

My father and my brothers, Dhrishtadyumna and Shikhandi, swore allegiance to the Pandavas and gifted us with gold, chariots, horses, elephants, and servants.

I am honoured that my daughter is wedded into the Kuru dynasty. Your illustrious ancestors are famous for their justice, wisdom, and prowess.

Draupadi, I have no doubt that the Kuru palace will give you all the respect, love, and care a woman deserves. You will be treated like a queen and guarded fiercely by your husbands.

Go fearlessly, sweet one, and be happy!

Those were my father's parting words to me...

...and what would my father say today? There sit my husbands, helpless and weak, unable to guard me.

Stung by my words, Bheema began to rise in anger, but Arjuna stopped him...

Bheema! We both want to kill every Kaurava we can lay our hands on. But now is **not** the time.

We are slaves to the Kauravas. Remember this for now.

Alas! Abiding by the rules of this foul game is more important to my lord Yudhishthira than his love for me and my honour!

He makes my other husbands powerless too!

Enough of this whining, Pandavas! As slaves you are forbidden from wearing your royal robes. Discard them now.

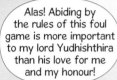

The sound of my lament tore through the stunned court.

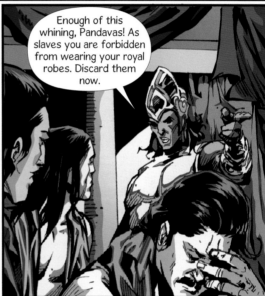

Though they seethed with anger, my husbands followed Karna's command.

And you, Draupadi. You are a slave too. Kindly follow your husbands' actions and surrender your clothing.

Karna was finally paying me back for my cruel words to him at my swayamvara. But disrobing a woman? What foul revenge was that?

Someone stop these mad men from insulting me!

I cried piteously, but Dushasana grabbed my clothes and began to disrobe me in the royal court of Hastinapur.

The Pandavas sobbed in frustration, unable to help their wife. Vidura, Bheeshma, and Dronacharya wept in shame. Yet not one man stood up to help me.

Aware that Dushasana was too strong for me and it was futile to fight him off, I lifted my hands up in surrender and prayed to Krishna with all my heart.

Krishna! Krishna! You alone are my saviour. Protect my honour!

Dushasana tugged at my robe, pulling persistently.

But Krishna, my unfailing divine friend, answered my prayers. While the court gaped in wonder, my robe multiplied endlessly. The more cloth Dushasana pulled with his big hands, the larger grew the pile of fabric at his feet. No matter how much cloth he wrenched off my body, there was always enough to cover me.

Drenched in sweat, Dushasana gasped for breath and collapsed in exhaustion as my never-ending silk piled higher and higher behind him.

The hall was still silent when Dushasana finally released his hold on my robes.

I lay crumpled on the floor. My self-respect shattered, my spirit broken. For a woman to have even an inch of her clothing forcibly pulled and stripped causes as deep and grievous a wound to her as the death stab of a sword in the flesh of a warrior.

I am convinced, Lady Draupadi, that even the gods do not wish for you to be a slave. Hence, I shall make you an offer you cannot refuse...

...I deem you free to marry any man you choose amongst us. Come, this is where you belong. I will care for you far better than these worthless husbands of yours.

That drove Bheema to the brink of mad rage. His brothers were not far behind. The Pandavas' patience had run out, and they swore to avenge my insult.

I heard Duryodhana pat his thigh as he spoke those words.

You will pay for these insults, Duryodhana! I swear by all that is sacred that I will break that thigh of yours in a duel.

And you, Dushasana, I swear I will tear you apart and drink your blood!

And I, Arjuna, vow that Karna will meet his end by my hands.

I, Sahadeva, will bring death to Shakuni.

And I, Nakula, vow to kill all these men who support Duryodhana.

The hall reverberated with the sound of those terrible oaths. The heavens showered blessings on the four Pandava brothers. By causing the oaths to be taken, I, the fire-born Draupadi, began fulfilling my mission on earth.

I had to suffer the loss of my dignity to reveal the true, dark nature of the Kauravas. Through my pain I tore the blindfold off the eyes of the Pandavas, reminding them of their own destiny – the destruction of evil.

Empowered by my husbands' fearsome vows, I glared at the court, and my bitter voice cut through the assembly.

This court of Hastinapur is not a council of wisdom. It is a nest of sin! The elders do not condemn what is wrong. They do not uphold what is virtuous.

For the suffering I have been through in this accursed court, I, Draupadi, the fire born lay a cu—

STOP!!!

Stop Draupadi! I beg you!

I knew that voice. All eyes turned towards the woman who had rushed into the hall. It was Queen Gandhari, mother of the Kauravas.

For the love of the gods! I beg you! Please do not curse this kingdom! Please do not curse the Kuru house!

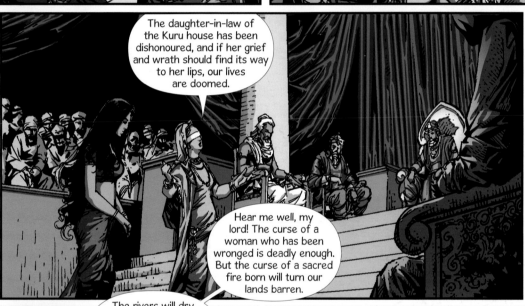

The daughter-in-law of the Kuru house has been dishonoured, and if her grief and wrath should find its way to her lips, our lives are doomed.

Hear me well, my lord! The curse of a woman who has been wronged is deadly enough. But the curse of a sacred fire born will turn our lands barren.

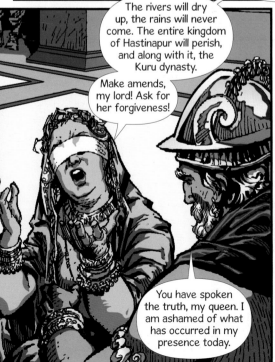

The rivers will dry up, the rains will never come. The entire kingdom of Hastinapur will perish, and along with it, the Kuru dynasty.

Make amends, my lord! Ask for her forgiveness!

You have spoken the truth, my queen. I am ashamed of what has occurred in my presence today.

Gripped by fear, Dhritarashtra knew this day had sealed the destruction of his house. To appease the wronged Pandavas, he hurried to make amends by being generous with us.

Draupadi, we have been cowards and have witnessed events that should never have taken place. If you can, please forgive me – forgive us. We offer our deepest apologies.

Please ask for what you wish.

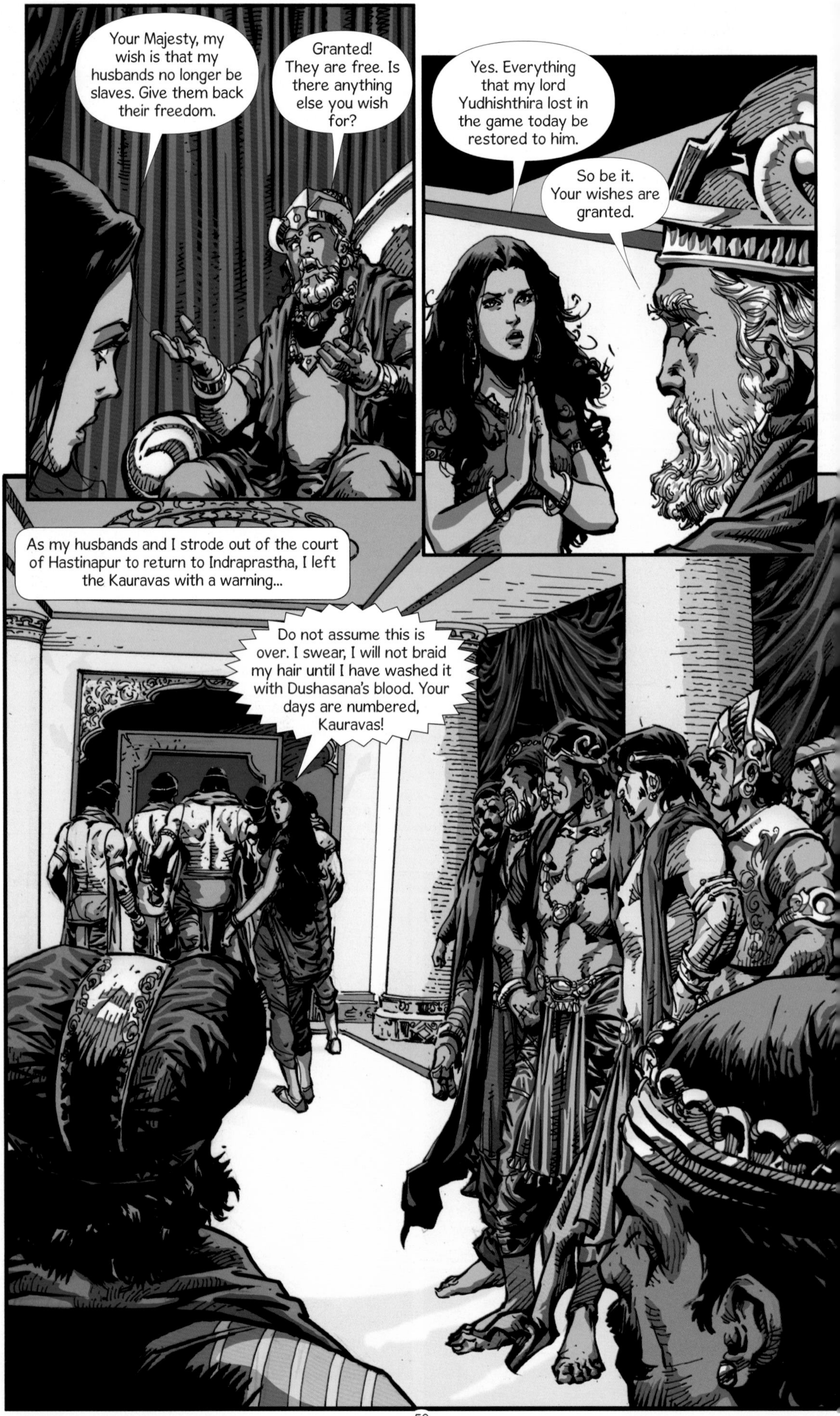

Your Majesty, my wish is that my husbands no longer be slaves. Give them back their freedom.
Granted! They are free. Is there anything else you wish for?
Yes. Everything that my lord Yudhishthira lost in the game today be restored to him.
So be it. Your wishes are granted.
As my husbands and I strode out of the court of Hastinapur to return to Indraprastha, I left the Kauravas with a warning...
Do not assume this is over. I swear, I will not braid my hair until I have washed it with Dushasana's blood. Your days are numbered, Kauravas!

We had left, but Duryodhana was livid with rage.

Father! What have you done? I won Indraprastha in the game. But due to your ridiculous generosity, it has gone back to the Pandavas.

Did you not hear their threats? Do you not see that the Pandavas will declare war on us as soon as they reach Indraprastha? Do you not care for the lives of your people and your sons?

Duryodhana! Do you not under--

Gandhari! You should stay out of this now.

You are right, Son. I did not think of this possibility. The Pandavas will now fulfil those terrible oaths they took.

What must I do now?

Before they reach Indraprastha, invite them again, to a second game of dice.

I know Yudhishthira. He loves the game far too much. He will come back to play and prove his skill. Moreover, he cannot refuse his uncle's invitation. His righteousness will not allow him to do so.

The rules of the game will be clear this time...

...the winner of this second game of dice will keep both Indraprastha and Hastinapur.

And the loser?

The loser will go into exile for thirteen years. The thirteenth year of exile must be lived in disguise. If the disguise is discovered, then the penalty is another thirteen years of exile.

Surely you are not considering playing again! I just want to go back to my palace. My sons are waiting for me.

But to my utter amazement, Yudhishthira ordered us back to Hastinapur for a second game of dice.

I do not understand why this game has to be played again. With Uncle Shakuni rolling the dice, the odds are against us.

Fate is cruel - I was back in the very court where I had been grievously insulted. Under my watchful gaze, a new game began.

Well, Yudhishthira, do you think you can keep your half of the kingdom safe from me? I always get what I desire.

Expert as he was, Shakuni threw the dice with much dexterity. And the inevitable happened.

Yes! I have won the first round.

Fortune did not smile on Yudhishthira even in the second round.

You have lost this round too, Yudhishthira!

HA HA

This is the final round. Will luck favour my lord this time?

But it was not to be. I could not look at Yudhishthira for days after that, for my anger would blaze in my eyes.

We have won! Dear nephew, we have won.

You have done it, Uncle Shakuni! I am now the lord of the entire kingdom!

Uncle Vidura spoke.

It is with a heavy heart that I declare this. As per the rules of the game, the Pandavas and their queen must forfeit their share of the kingdom, and their wealth and servants. From this day, for thirteen years, they are exiled to the forest.

Our beautiful Indraprastha was surrendered to the Kauravas. Queen Kunti was entrusted to the care of Uncle Vidura, and my sons were sent to the palace of Panchala.

Abandoning all luxury, the Pandavas and I set out on our journey.

The kingdom bid a tearful farewell to its rightful and favourite rulers.

People assembled there said that though the Pandavas had been stripped of all their wealth and glory, they still shone like gods. And I, bereft of my royal jewellery and silks, still glowed like the goddess Shree herself.

But I was not concerned with our appearance. I felt humiliated, and my silent fury was visible as I followed my husbands into exile.

THE EXILE

Accompanied by several Brahmins, my husbands and I found our way to the Kamyaka forest.

But in the forest, how would we ensure the well-being of so many people?

Rishi Dhaumya, please advise me on how we may provide food for these revered Brahmins who are now under our protection.

The true provider of nourishment in our world is Surya, the sun god. Worship him. He will assist you.

This beautiful forest is where we will begin our exile. Please return to Hastinapur, where you will all be looked after by my cousin Duryodhana.

We have no desire to return to a city where evil rules and righteousness is forgotten. We shall also reside in this forest with you.

Yudhishthira acted on Rishi Dhaumya's advice. Pleased with his devotion, the brightly shining Surya appeared before him.

My gift to you is this *akshayapatra*. This sacred bowl will provide the tastiest food for as many people as Draupadi wishes to serve at each meal.

I am most grateful, Lord Surya.

The vessel gifted by Surya would always hold food when I served from it...

...and would only be empty once I had eaten my share.

Thus the Pandavas and I were able to fulfil our duty as Kshatriyas to provide food for the Brahmins.

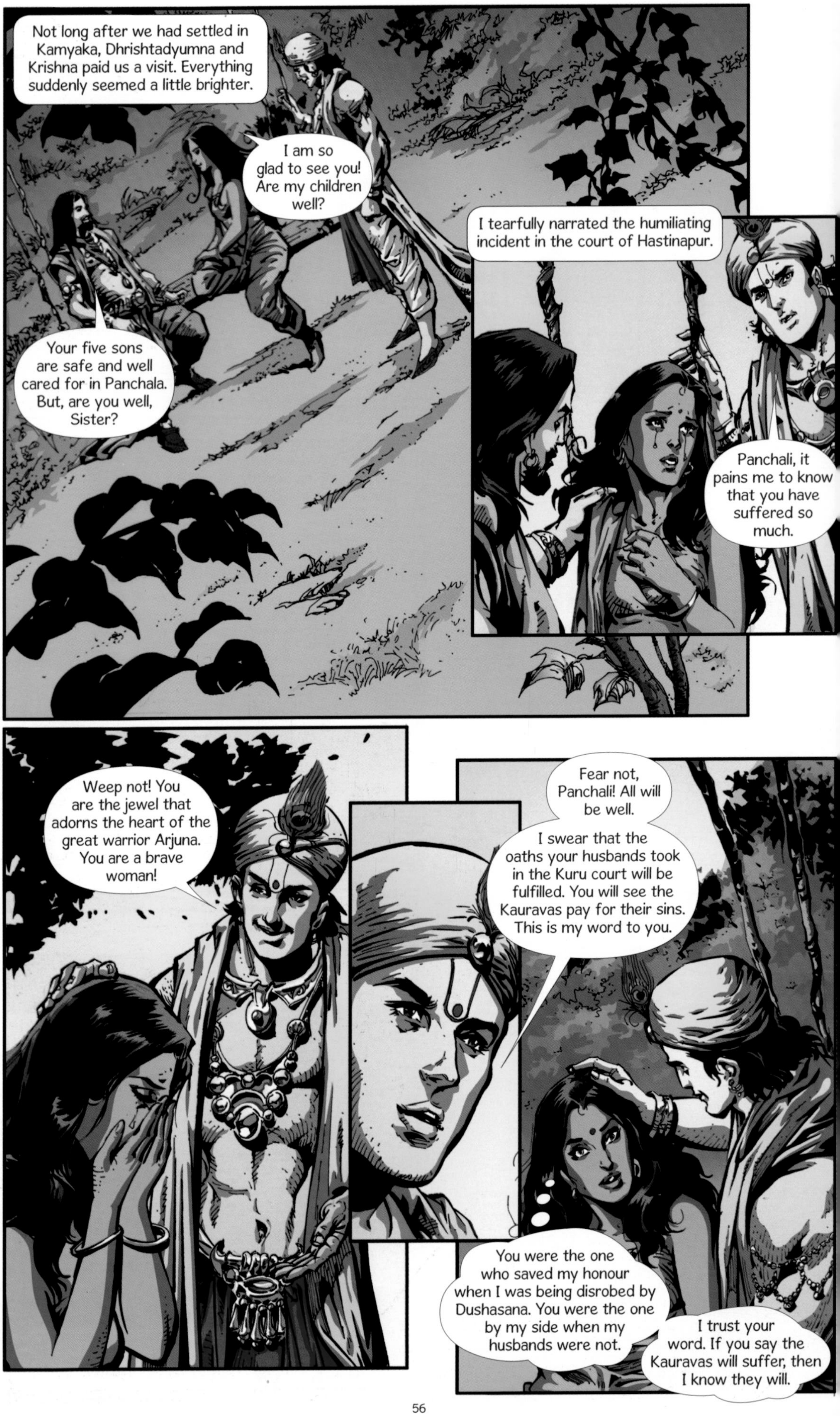

Not long after we had settled in Kamyaka, Dhrishtadyumna and Krishna paid us a visit. Everything suddenly seemed a little brighter.
I am so glad to see you! Are my children well?
Your five sons are safe and well cared for in Panchala. But, are you well, Sister?
I tearfully narrated the humiliating incident in the court of Hastinapur.
Panchali, it pains me to know that you have suffered so much.
Weep not! You are the jewel that adorns the heart of the great warrior Arjuna. You are a brave woman!
Fear not, Panchali! All will be well.
I swear that the oaths your husbands took in the Kuru court will be fulfilled. You will see the Kauravas pay for their sins. This is my word to you.
You were the one who saved my honour when I was being disrobed by Dushasana. You were the one by my side when my husbands were not.
I trust your word. If you say the Kauravas will suffer, then I know they will.

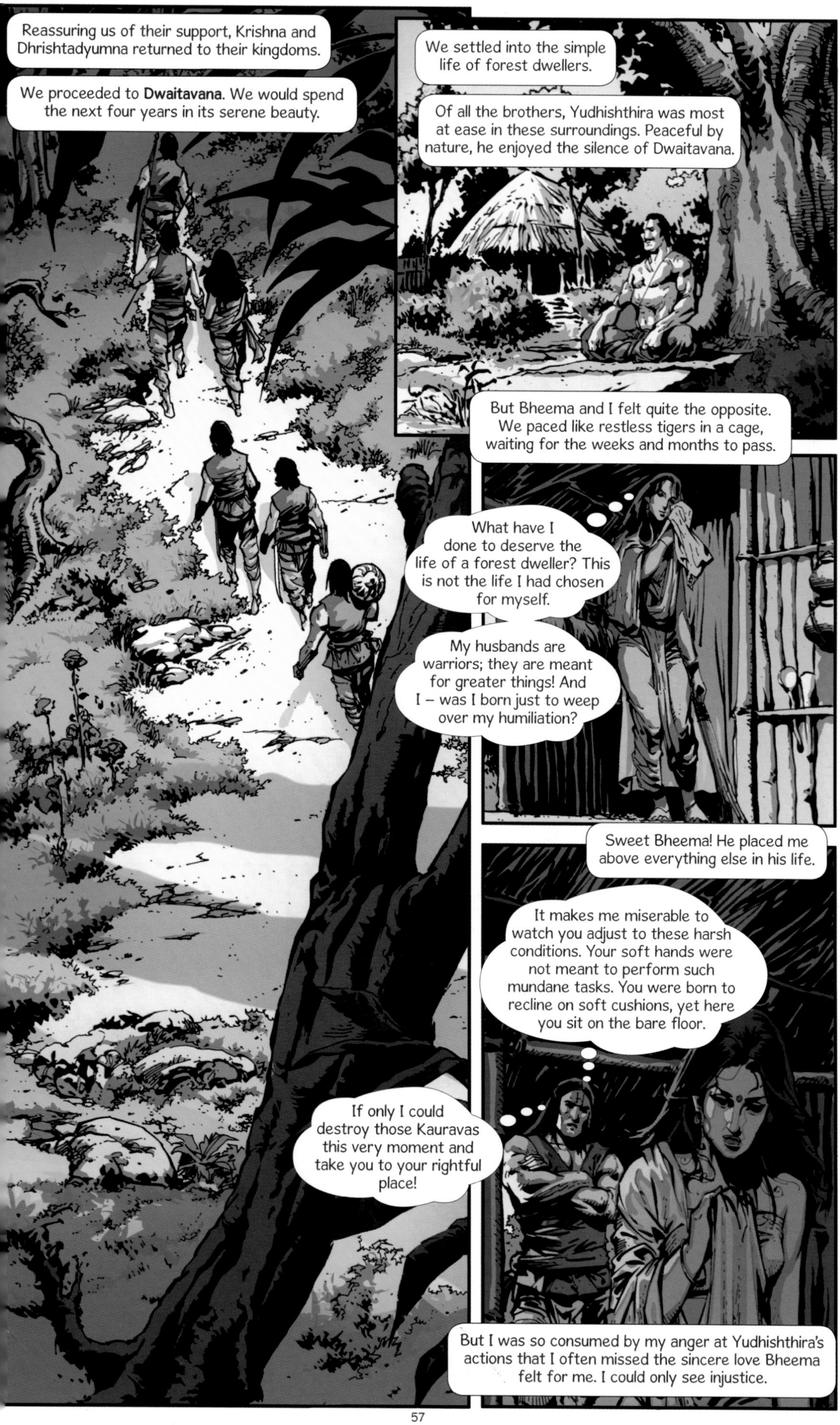

Reassuring us of their support, Krishna and Dhrishtadyumna returned to their kingdoms.
We proceeded to **Dwaitavana**. We would spend the next four years in its serene beauty.
We settled into the simple life of forest dwellers.
Of all the brothers, Yudhishthira was most at ease in these surroundings. Peaceful by nature, he enjoyed the silence of Dwaitavana.
But Bheema and I felt quite the opposite. We paced like restless tigers in a cage, waiting for the weeks and months to pass.
What have I done to deserve the life of a forest dweller? This is not the life I had chosen for myself.
My husbands are warriors; they are meant for greater things! And I – was I born just to weep over my humiliation?
Sweet Bheema! He placed me above everything else in his life.
It makes me miserable to watch you adjust to these harsh conditions. Your soft hands were not meant to perform such mundane tasks. You were born to recline on soft cushions, yet here you sit on the bare floor.
If only I could destroy those Kauravas this very moment and take you to your rightful place!
But I was so consumed by my anger at Yudhishthira's actions that I often missed the sincere love Bheema felt for me. I could only see injustice.

One night, unable to bear it any longer, I finally spoke my mind.

Come Draupadi! Watch how lovely--

I am not as patient as you, son of Dharma. The beauty of the night cannot soothe the pain of my humiliation at the hands of the Kauravas.

I am a woman of royal blood, and I do not take insults to my honour with ease. But what the Kauravas did was beyond what any woman, royal or common, should endure in her life.

Draupadi, this is a time for patience.

What patience? I do not understand this patience! The truth is that your love for dharma is far greater than your love for our family!

As my husband and my king, you are not ready to fight for my honour or our family's honour. What sort of Kshatriya are you? You have lost your spirit. To me, you have lost the right to call yourself a warrior.

Draupadi, I am the son of Dharma. I am an ascetic at heart. I do not care for worldly pleasures.

But you... you are the beautiful daughter of Fire, and like fire you are impulsive, restless, and hungry for justice.

I hold myself responsible for bringing you here. Know that I too am pained each moment I see you suffer this harsh forest life.

However, now is **not** the time to pick up weapons to fight Duryodhana. I will keep my word and follow my dharma. I **will** complete these thirteen years of exile...

...but **after** that, the Kauravas will see the true Kshatriya in me. They will be punished as they deserve to be.

I felt somewhat reassured to finally hear Yudhishthira speak thus. I fell silent. But deep inside, my spirit still simmered, aching for revenge.

I will hold you to your words, Yudhishthira!

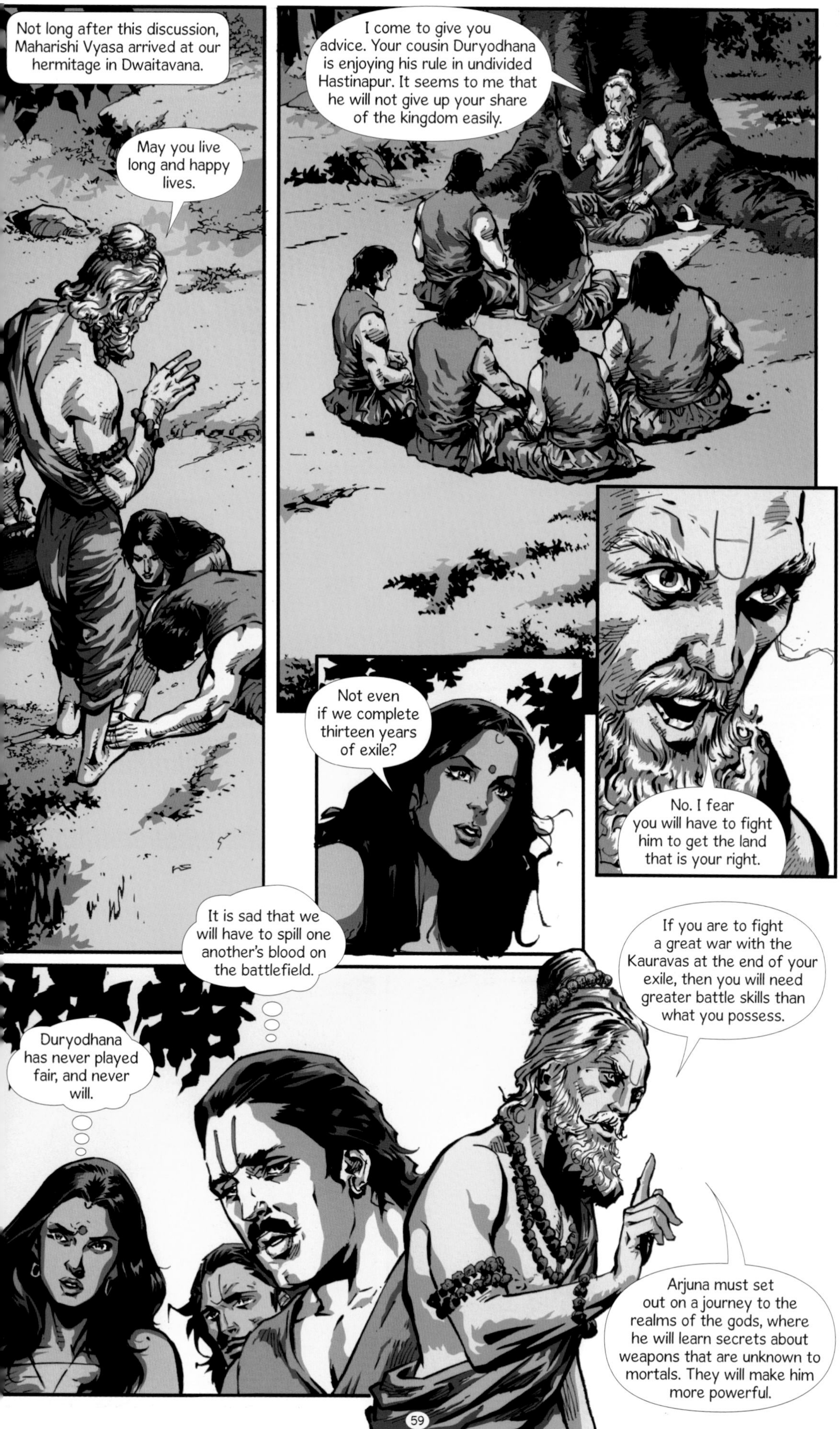
Not long after this discussion, Maharishi Vyasa arrived at our hermitage in Dwaitavana.
May you live long and happy lives.
I come to give you advice. Your cousin Duryodhana is enjoying his rule in undivided Hastinapur. It seems to me that he will not give up your share of the kingdom easily.
Not even if we complete thirteen years of exile?
No. I fear you will have to fight him to get the land that is your right.
It is sad that we will have to spill one another's blood on the battlefield.
Duryodhana has never played fair, and never will.
If you are to fight a great war with the Kauravas at the end of your exile, then you will need greater battle skills than what you possess.
Arjuna must set out on a journey to the realms of the gods, where he will learn secrets about weapons that are unknown to mortals. They will make him more powerful.

Go Arjuna! Spend this time wisely and try to acquire all the weapons you can.

May it be so, Maharishi Vyasa.

After blessing Arjuna, the great sage departed.

I was heartbroken to see Arjuna leave. Even before I had met and married him, he held a special place in my heart. Our parting was tender.

Return soon, Arjuna.

Beloved Draupadi, stay safe until then.

Without Arjuna, Dwaitavana has suddenly lost its charm.

Why do we not spend some time travelling? I have a great desire to visit the holy pilgrimage spots.

We must do exactly that, Sahadeva. It will soothe Draupadi's heart. She aches at being separated from Arjuna.

So the four Pandava brothers and I visited several sacred sites.

After some years, we finally proceeded north to the Himalayas where we were reunited with Arjuna.

Ten long years of exile were over. We returned to Kamyaka forest to spend the last few years of our exile.

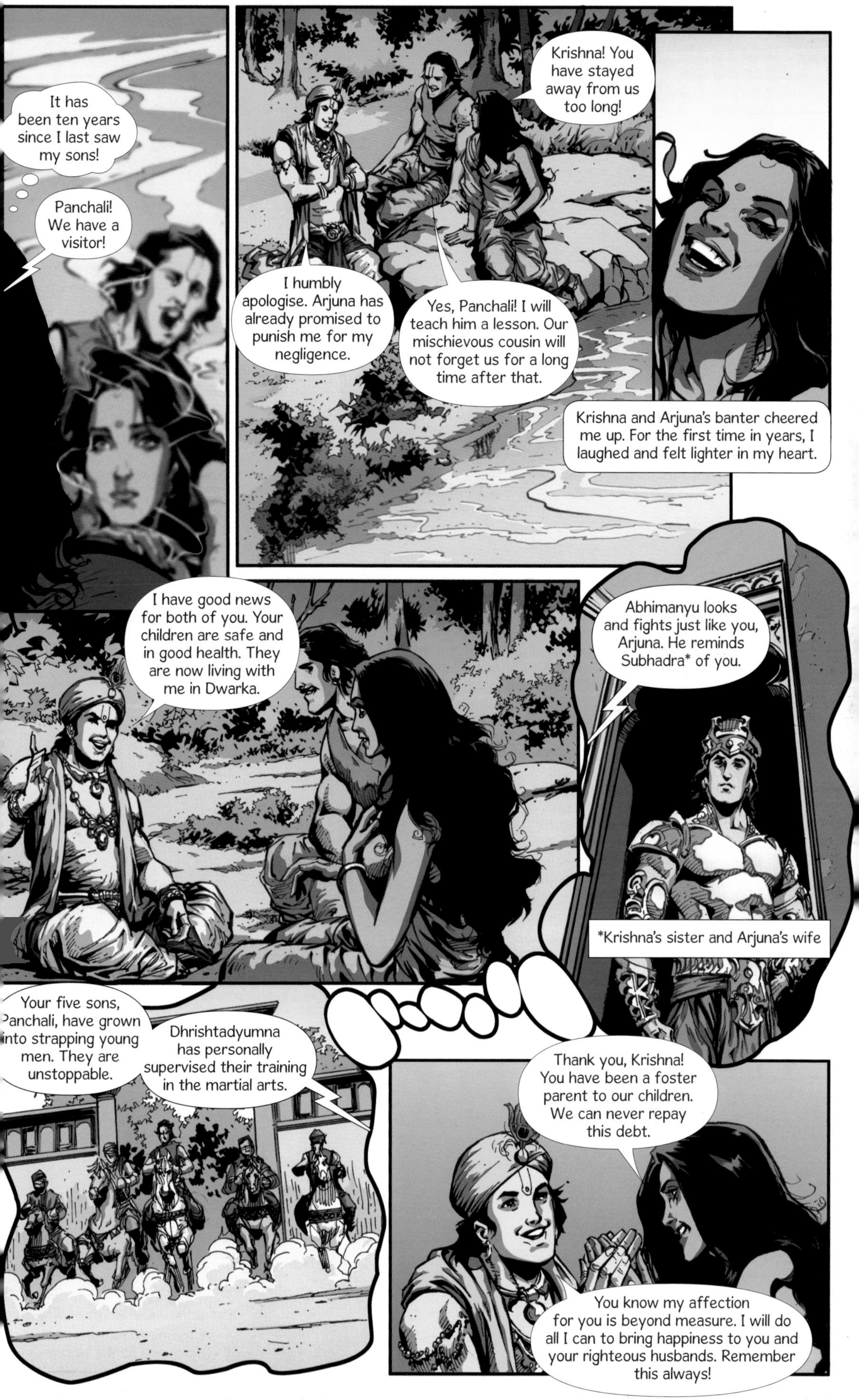
It has been ten years since I last saw my sons!
Panchali! We have a visitor!
Krishna! You have stayed away from us too long!
I humbly apologise. Arjuna has already promised to punish me for my negligence.
Yes, Panchali! I will teach him a lesson. Our mischievous cousin will not forget us for a long time after that.
Krishna and Arjuna's banter cheered me up. For the first time in years, I laughed and felt lighter in my heart.
I have good news for both of you. Your children are safe and in good health. They are now living with me in Dwarka.
Abhimanyu looks and fights just like you, Arjuna. He reminds Subhadra* of you.
*Krishna's sister and Arjuna's wife
Your five sons, Panchali, have grown into strapping young men. They are unstoppable.
Dhrishtadyumna has personally supervised their training in the martial arts.
Thank you, Krishna! You have been a foster parent to our children. We can never repay this debt.
You know my affection for you is beyond measure. I will do all I can to bring happiness to you and your righteous husbands. Remember this always!

There is news from Hastinapur too--

Tell us, Krishna. How is our mother? How are our cousins and Kuru elders? Are they well?

Queen Kunti is well taken care of by your uncle Vidura. Duryodhana on the other hand...

...has found a useful friend in Karna. The mighty Karna conquered the kings who defied Duryodhana's authority.

Other kings submitted to Duryodhana's rule. He is now hailed as the most powerful ruler.

Desperate to match your fame, Duryodhana wanted to perform the rajasuya yajna too. But as per the laws of that yajna, as a crown prince with a living father, he could not do so. Instead, he has performed the *vaishnava* yajna and is now considered invincible.

We digested the news silently. The very thought of the evil Duryodhana ruling unjustly was repulsive.

I have told you all I know. I must now return to Dwarka.

I carry your blessings for your sons. You shall see them soon, Panchali. Be strong!

Keep them safe, Krishna! I fear something terrible is going to occur soon.

My premonition came true. In the safety of the hermitage, evil found me again...

It was the twelfth year of exile. One morning, Rishi Dhaumya and I bade farewell to the Pandavas as they left on their daily hunting trip.

We shall be back by midday.

Goodbye, Draupadi! I shall bring you the purple flowers I promised.

Stay safe, my husbands!

That same morning, Jayadratha, the king of Sindhu, was journeying through the Kamyaka forest towards the kingdom of Salva.

A hermitage? In this wilderness?

Take me closer!

As they neared the hermitage, Jayadratha spotted me. I was unaware that I was being watched.

Born with the gift of loveliness, she stands so gracefully! Such a perfect face! Such incredible beauty! Is she a goddess? But I feel I have seen this face before...

Unable to hold back his adoration, Jayadratha dismounted and approached me.

Bewitching maiden! I am Jayadratha, king of Sindhu.

I am eager to know who you are. Are you a celestial dancer fallen from the heavens? Or are you Goddess Shree herself?

King Jayadratha is Princess Dushala's husband. This means that he is Uncle Dhritarashtra's son-in-law and my brother-in-law!

I introduced myself as the wife of the Pandavas, cousins of Dushala.

My husbands are away hunting. If you wait a few hours, they will return and welcome you appropriately.

Jayadratha could not take his eyes off me. I felt threatened by his direct gaze, and my heart thudded with fear.

So **you** are the beautiful Draupadi. I thought I had seen you before.

I beg you! Leave those worthless Pandavas and this harsh forest. Become my queen, and all my treasures, palaces, and lands will be yours!

Foolish man! You insult my husbands! The Pandavas will make you suffer for your audacity. Go back to your wife, before they return.

You dare refuse **me**! Ungrateful woman!

AAAAHHHHH!

Help! Bheema! Arjuna!

Though I fought him, Jayadratha was too powerful for me. He bundled me into his chariot and departed swiftly, his army following behind him.

My cries brought Rishi Dhaumya out of the hut. But it was too late. Jayadratha's chariot had already disappeared into the distance. Just then the Pandavas returned.

What is that cloud of dust?

I sensed something was wrong, so we returned early. Where is Draupadi?

On being told of my abduction, Arjuna and Bheema raced through the forest in pursuit of Jayadratha...

...and soon caught up with the king of Sindhu.

Jayadratha's army was routed by the fearsome skills of the two Pandavas alone.

Stunned and frightened, Jayadratha could only stare.

A terrified Jayadratha scrambled away to save his life.

But Arjuna and Bheema gave chase.

Who are these men?

My husbands, Bheema and Arjuna. For you, they are the angels of death, come to destroy you, just as I said they would.

You coward, Jayadratha! Come back and fight like a man!

They caught him, bound him, and...

...shaved the hair off his head. Fearful for his life, Jayadratha begged for mercy.

Bheema and Arjuna left it to Yudhishthira to decide what punishment lay in store for him.

SNIP!

You have committed a grave mistake by casting your eye on Drapaudi, and kidnapping her.

Any other man in my place would have chopped your head off this instant. However, you are the husband of my cousin Dushala and the son-in-law of Queen Gandhari. By killing you, I would cause both these women tremendous grief.

Therefore, Jayadratha, I shall spare your life. Go, return in peace to your wife and your kingdom.

I watched as Jayadratha walked away a free man. My pride had been hurt once again, and I shed hot, angry tears.

That man was bold enough to kidnap your wife! Yet you forgave him? He should have been killed immediately. Yet all he received was your compassion!

Defeat is an even greater wound to a Kshatriya's pride than death.

Would you want young Dushala to be widowed?

Much as I despised that question, it was a just one. So I swallowed the bitter anger that clutched at my throat.

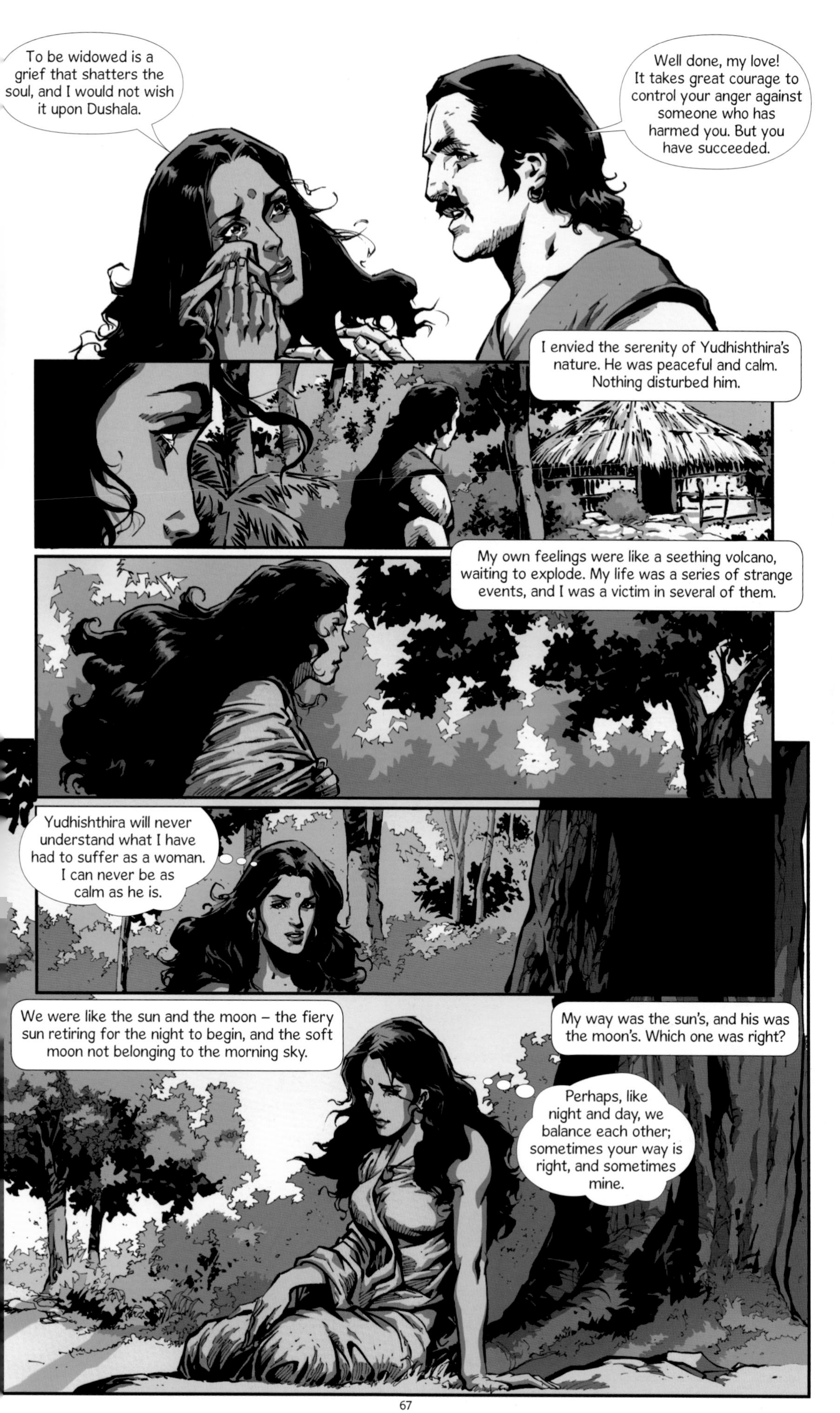
To be widowed is a grief that shatters the soul, and I would not wish it upon Dushala.
Well done, my love! It takes great courage to control your anger against someone who has harmed you. But you have succeeded.
I envied the serenity of Yudhishthira's nature. He was peaceful and calm. Nothing disturbed him.
My own feelings were like a seething volcano, waiting to explode. My life was a series of strange events, and I was a victim in several of them.
Yudhishthira will never understand what I have had to suffer as a woman. I can never be as calm as he is.
We were like the sun and the moon – the fiery sun retiring for the night to begin, and the soft moon not belonging to the morning sky.
My way was the sun's, and his was the moon's. Which one was right?
Perhaps, like night and day, we balance each other; sometimes your way is right, and sometimes mine.

The thirteenth year of exile dawned. It was the year we had to live in disguise.

I have heard that King Virata rules the kingdom of Matsya. He is a soft-spoken, gentle man. We should all take up service in his palace.

I agree. This is a sound plan. No one will think of looking for us in Matsya.

Yes, yes! We all agree.

Draupadi, are you happy with this plan?

My husbands and I are to be servants in the palace of Virata? I would never be happy with such a plan. But, if it is the safest way to complete our last year of exile, I will accept it.

We travelled to Matsya in disguise and sought employment with King Virata.

Impressed with the skill and natural charm of the five brothers, Virata immediately took them into his palace.

In the twelve years of exile, Yudhishthira had mastered the art of throwing dice. He disguised himself as a Brahmin named Kanka, and taught King Virata the intricacies of the game, soon becoming his close companion.

Bheema, who loved food, had disguised himself as Ballava, and was appointed chief cook in Virata's palace kitchens. In his spare time, he also taught wrestling in the royal gymnasium.

During his stay in the land of the gods, Arjuna had not only acquired magical weapons, but had also learnt how to dance, sing, and play instruments. While there, he had also been unfortunate to incur the wrath of Urvashi, a celestial dancer, who cursed him to lead a life of a eunuch for a year.

So Arjuna became Brihannalaa, a eunuch and teacher of dance and music, responsible for instructing Princess Uttaraa in the arts.

Sahadeva knew every breed of cow and exactly what care each animal needed to yield the best milk. He disguised himself as Tantripala, and became the chief of Virata's cowsheds.

Nakula was the equestrian of the family. He became Damagranthi and took charge of the royal stables, tending to the horses with care and expertise.

And I...

...dressed as a handmaiden, requested an audience with Queen Sudeshna, wife of Virata.

My name is Malini. I was once the royal maid to Queen Draupadi of Indraprastha, and I am looking for a new mistress to serve.

I can decorate your hair in a hundred different ways.

I can create the sweetest perfumes to soothe your senses and cool your skin.

I can also make flower garlands of matchless beauty to adorn your wrists, ankles, and braids.

Sudeshna was charmed by my talents. But she had her doubts.

You are far too beautiful. I am afraid that the men in this palace will all vie for your attention. Your presence may cause trouble.

I am married to five powerful demigods. I cannot live with them because they are under a curse for one year. However, if any man dares lay a finger on me, my husbands will destroy him.

I promise not to disturb the peace of your kingdom. I will stay away from the court so that the king and his men never set eyes on me.

Very well then, Malini. You shall serve me from today.

I am grateful... Your Majesty.

Can my life get any more humiliating? I am now a maid to a minor queen.

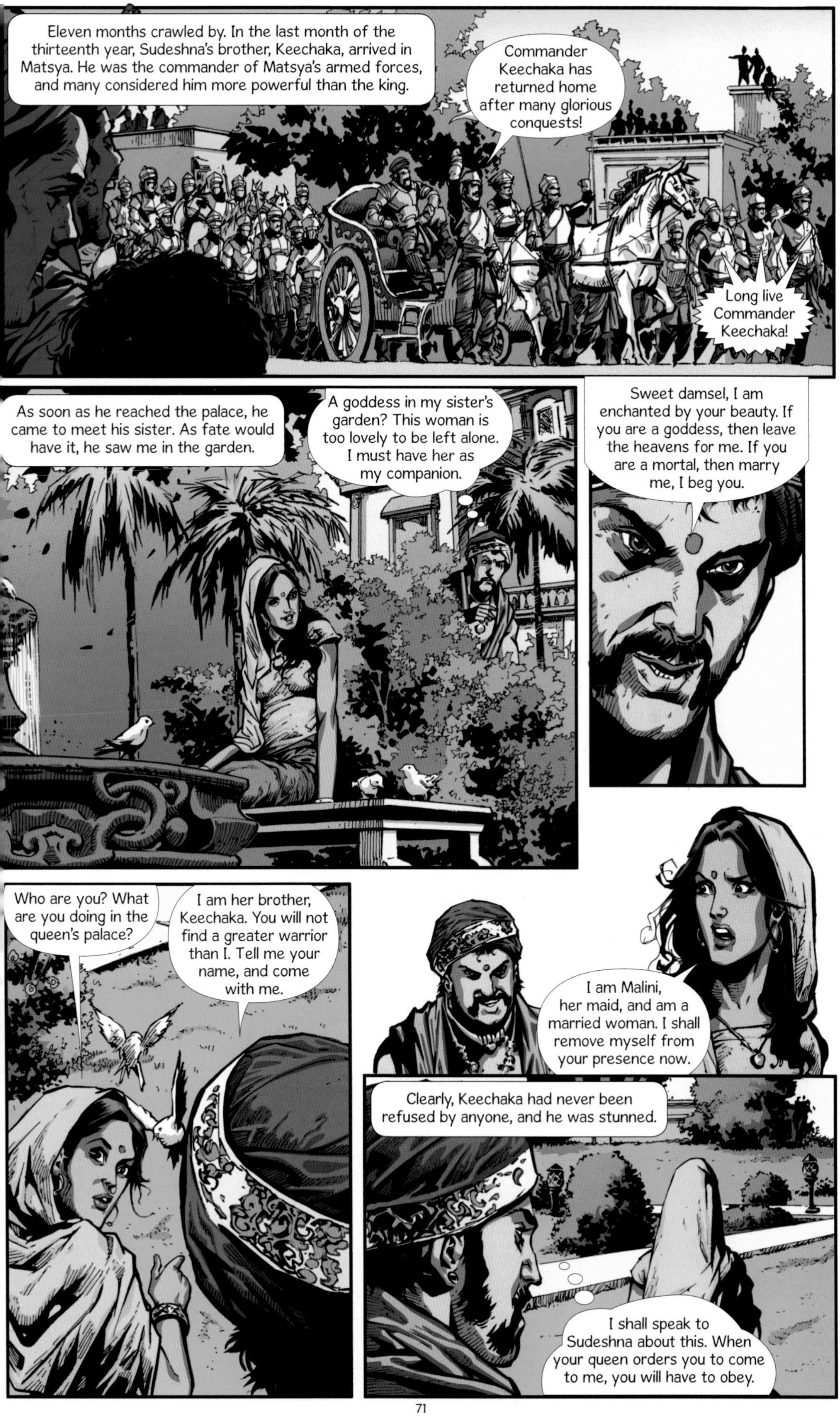

Eleven months crawled by. In the last month of the thirteenth year, Sudeshna's brother, Keechaka, arrived in Matsya. He was the commander of Matsya's armed forces, and many considered him more powerful than the king.
Commander Keechaka has returned home after many glorious conquests!
Long live Commander Keechaka!
As soon as he reached the palace, he came to meet his sister. As fate would have it, he saw me in the garden.
A goddess in my sister's garden? This woman is too lovely to be left alone. I must have her as my companion.
Sweet damsel, I am enchanted by your beauty. If you are a goddess, then leave the heavens for me. If you are a mortal, then marry me, I beg you.
Who are you? What are you doing in the queen's palace?
I am her brother, Keechaka. You will not find a greater warrior than I. Tell me your name, and come with me.
I am Malini, her maid, and am a married woman. I shall remove myself from your presence now.
Clearly, Keechaka had never been refused by anyone, and he was stunned.
I shall speak to Sudeshna about this. When your queen orders you to come to me, you will have to obey.

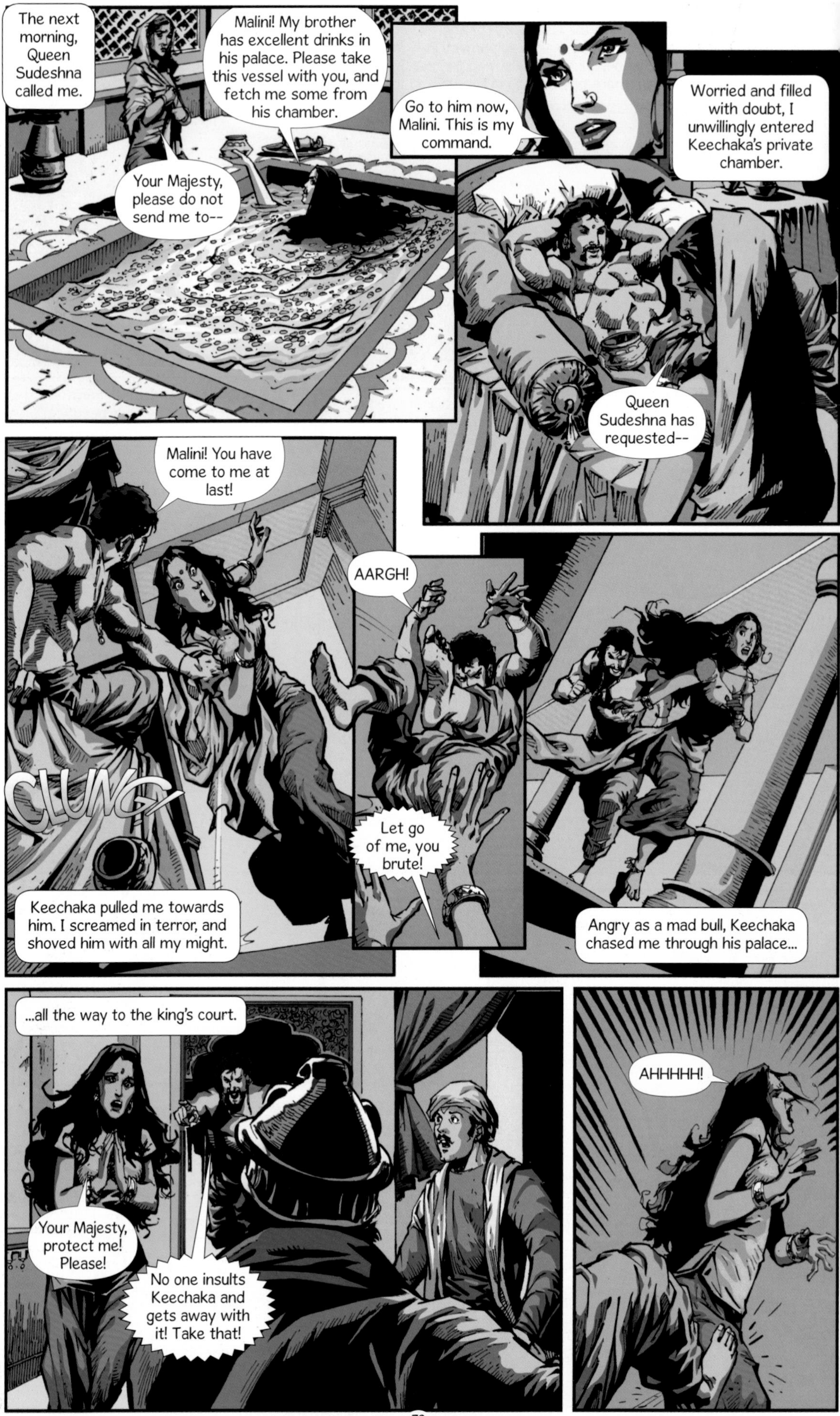
The next morning, Queen Sudeshna called me.
Malini! My brother has excellent drinks in his palace. Please take this vessel with you, and fetch me some from his chamber.
Your Majesty, please do not send me to--
Go to him now, Malini. This is my command.
Worried and filled with doubt, I unwillingly entered Keechaka's private chamber.
Queen Sudeshna has requested--
Malini! You have come to me at last!
CLUNG!
Keechaka pulled me towards him. I screamed in terror, and shoved him with all my might.
AARGH!
Let go of me, you brute!
Angry as a mad bull, Keechaka chased me through his palace...
...all the way to the king's court.
Your Majesty, protect me! Please!
No one insults Keechaka and gets away with it! Take that!
AHHHHH!

King Virata was afraid of the commander of his army. Despite my piteous sobs, Virata remained silent as Keechaka stomped off.

Let this be a lesson for you!

Yudhishthira turned white with fury, but spoke in a gentle tone.

Do not cry. I have heard that only a fortnight remains for your husbands to be freed from the curse. Please wait patiently for them.

My eyes met my husband's.

Forgive me for not protecting you! The king must not suspect that we know each other.

Why do you fail me again and again?

My patience has run out. If I could kill Keechaka myself, I would do it this moment.

Without saying a word to anyone, I left the court, and...

...went to Bheema.

You must destroy that vile creature. I am unsafe in this city as long as he is alive.

Leave it to me. I will crush him.

But for that you must...

As planned, I went to Keechaka.

I have changed my mind. Please meet me in the dance hall at midnight.

Excellent! I accept your invitation.

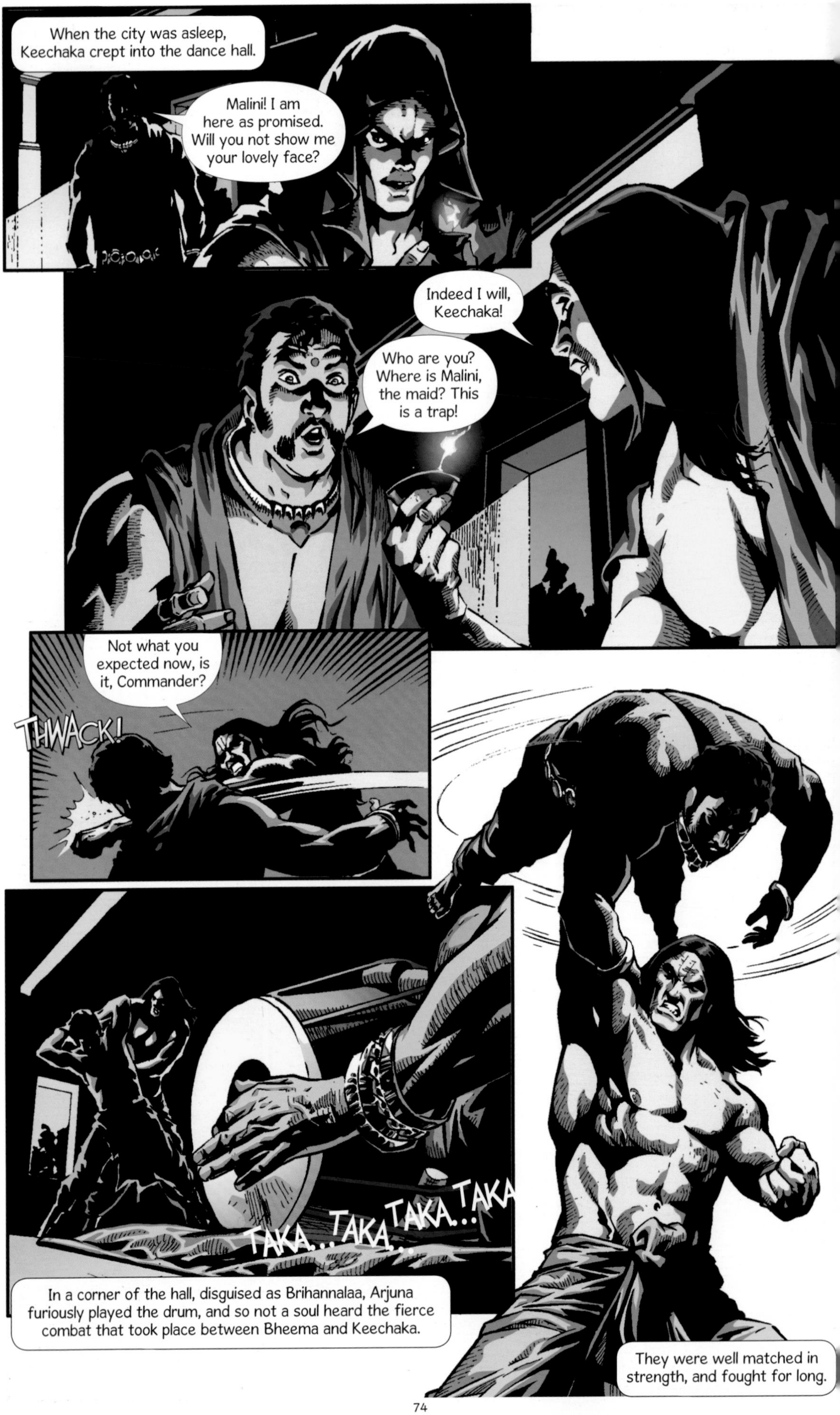

When the city was asleep, Keechaka crept into the dance hall.
Malini! I am here as promised. Will you not show me your lovely face?
Indeed I will, Keechaka!
Who are you? Where is Malini, the maid? This is a trap!
Not what you expected now, is it, Commander?
THWACK!
TAKA...TAKA...TAKA...TAKA
In a corner of the hall, disguised as Brihannalaa, Arjuna furiously played the drum, and so not a soul heard the fierce combat that took place between Bheema and Keechaka.
They were well matched in strength, and fought for long.

But Bheema gained the upper hand...

This is to avenge your insult to my Draupadi.

TAKA TAKA... TAKA... TAKA... TAKA... TAKA...

...and Keechaka's twisted body lay still forever.

The next morning...

Alas, Malini! My brother is dead! Who could have killed Keechaka?

I had warned you that my husbands would slay any man who tried to harm me.

Malini! You calmly stand there and tell me your husbands killed my brother? I want you out of my palace, this moment!

I cannot leave now! We still have two weeks of our exile to complete.

Please, Your Majesty! Do not...

I will not hear a word! Leave, Malini!

I swallowed my pride and begged.

A fortnight is all I ask! I shall be gone from your life after that! Allow me to stay for a fortnight, Your Majesty!

If I do not agree to her request, her husbands might turn their wrath upon someone else in my family.

Very well, Malini. You may stay for a fortnight.

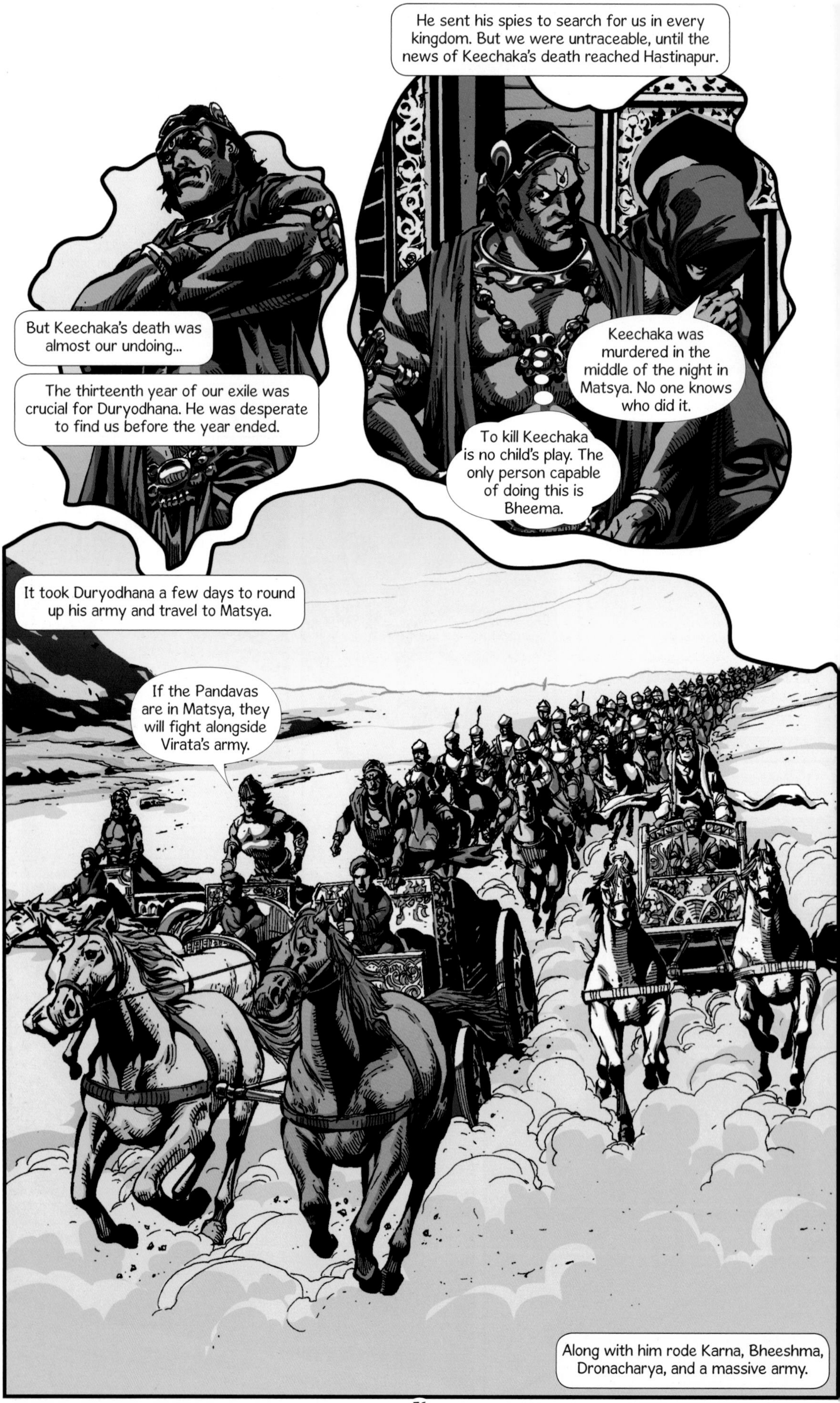
He sent his spies to search for us in every kingdom. But we were untraceable, until the news of Keechaka's death reached Hastinapur.
But Keechaka's death was almost our undoing...
The thirteenth year of our exile was crucial for Duryodhana. He was desperate to find us before the year ended.
Keechaka was murdered in the middle of the night in Matsya. No one knows who did it.
To kill Keechaka is no child's play. The only person capable of doing this is Bheema.
It took Duryodhana a few days to round up his army and travel to Matsya.
If the Pandavas are in Matsya, they will fight alongside Virata's army.
Along with him rode Karna, Bheeshma, Dronacharya, and a massive army.

Thirteen days of our last fortnight in Matsya had passed. On the morning of the fourteenth, from the queen's balcony, I heard a commotion in the street below.

The borders have been breached! Duryodhana of Hastinapur has attacked Matsya!

Hurry! Round up all the men you can find! The invading army is huge!

I rushed to a window and saw Arjuna mount the chariot of Prince Uttara, son of Virata.

Ride like the wind, Brihannalaa! We must make haste! Matsya must be defended at any cost.

Yes, Your Highness! Hold on tight!

Duryodhana must have suspected that we are hiding in Matsya. But in a few hours, our thirteenth year of exile will end. I hope he does not find us before that.

77

I paced up and down the chamber. If we were found out even one moment before the thirteenth year was up, we would have to spend another thirteen years in exile.

I watched the movement of the sun across the sky, eager for time to pass. A short while later, the resounding call of a conch shell rang through the city streets all the way to the palace balcony.

This is what I had been waiting for – and I broke into laughter. My heart fluttered with excitement.

PHHWWUUU!

That is the sound of Arjuna's conch shell! This is like music to my ears.

Since Arjuna has shed his disguise, it means that our exile has finally come to an end.

Krishna! Your blessings have helped us through this difficult year. I can now meet my sons, and delight in their company!

Relief flooded me. The fire-born princess was no longer a maid. I was once again Queen Draupadi, daughter-in-law of the royal house of Kuru.

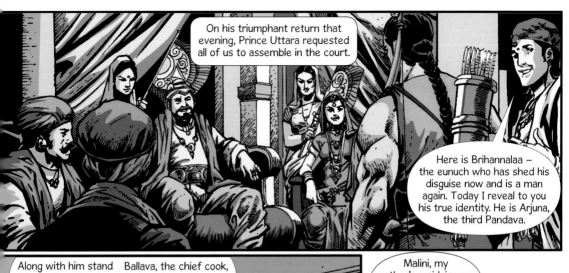

On his triumphant return that evening, Prince Uttara requested all of us to assemble in the court.

Here is Brihannalaa – the eunuch who has shed his disguise now and is a man again. Today I reveal to you his true identity. He is Arjuna, the third Pandava.

Along with him stand his brothers. Kanka, the noble Brahmin, is the famous King Yudhishthira.

Ballava, the chief cook, is the mighty Bheema. Damagranthi is Nakula, and Tantripala is Sahadeva.

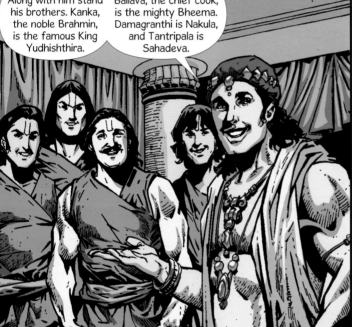

Malini, my mother's maid, is none other than Queen Draupadi, wife of the Pandavas.

Exclamations of astonishment rang through the court. Sudeshna was horrified.

Draupadi? Oh! What a terrible blunder I have committed by making her serve me!

They behaved with such humility that we never suspected their true identity.

We have committed a grave sin by treating these heroes as mere servants. For today, Matsya owes its freedom to Arjuna.

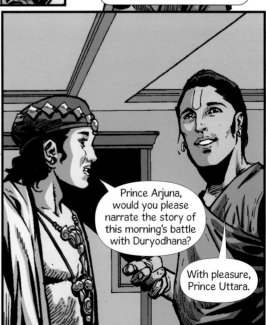

Prince Arjuna, would you please narrate the story of this morning's battle with Duryodhana?

With pleasure, Prince Uttara.

PHHWWUUU

Arjuna told us that he had blown his conch right after the thirteenth year of exile had ended.

He described how the furious Duryodhana had insisted on fighting, though he knew we had fulfilled all the conditions required of us.

Single-handedly, Arjuna had routed the entire army by making them faint under the spell of a magical weapon.

At the end of Arjuna's account, the court erupted in applause.

Long live Prince Arjuna! Long live Prince Uttara!

I took great satisfaction in Duryodhana's defeat.

I am honoured to be your wife, Arjuna.

King Virata was overwhelmed with the news.

Your Majesty! I am so ashamed. I have treated all of you as servants. Please forgive me!

Rise, King Virata! We should thank you, instead. You provided us with shelter in our thirteenth year of exile.

King Virata offered Princess Uttaraa in marriage to Arjuna, but my husband accepted her as a bride for his son, Abhimanyu.

Messengers were sent to Dwarka. Along with Krishna came Abhimanyu and my dear, dear sons.

In thirteen years, my sons had grown into young men! Each looked like a younger version of his father.

I have waited for this moment for so long!

The wedding of Abhimanyu and Uttaraa was celebrated with great pomp and glory.

After all this time, it is wonderful to be favoured by the gods again. I cannot wait to return home to Indraprastha.

It felt like the gods had remembered me, and were blessing us with the joy we deserved.

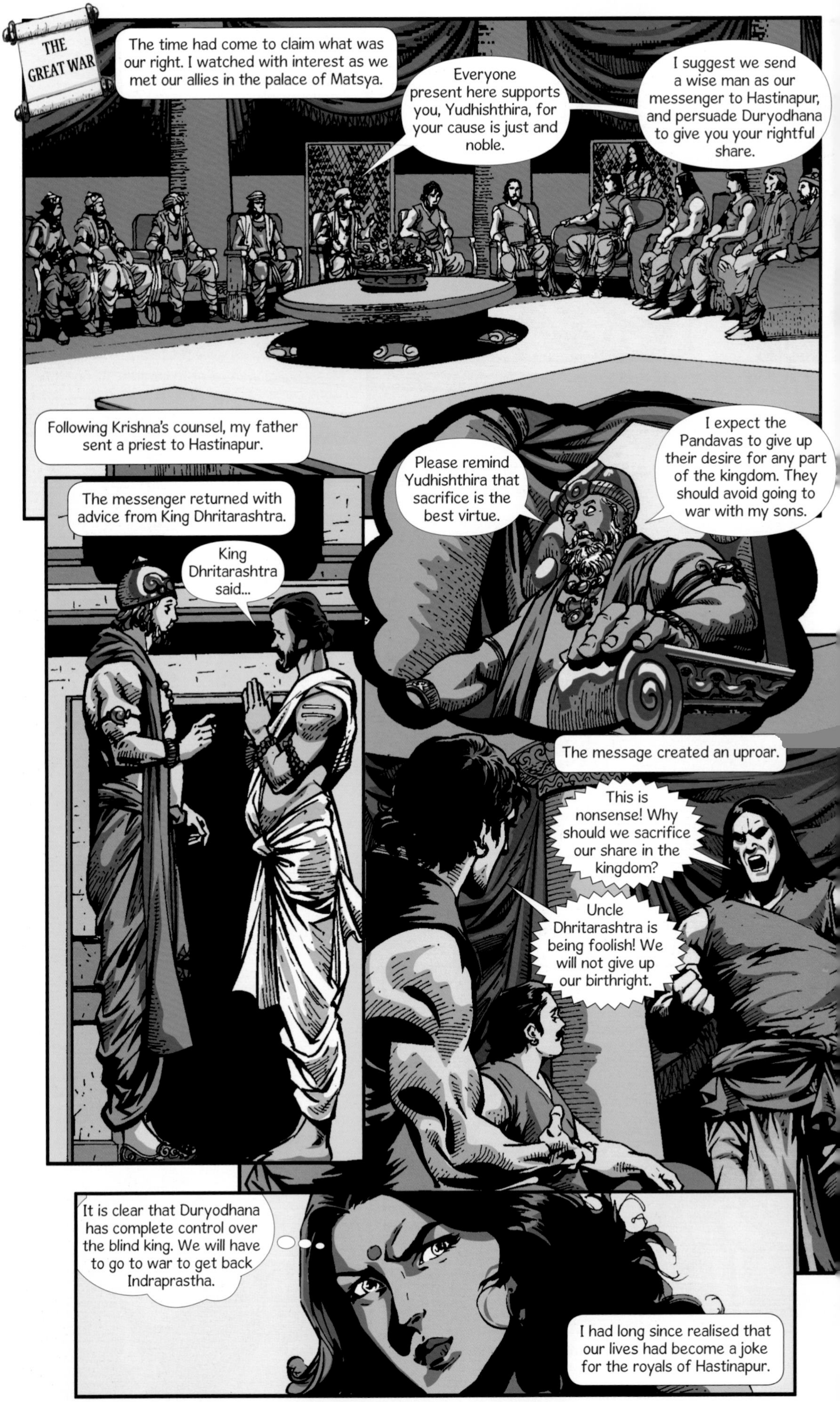
THE GREAT WAR
The time had come to claim what was our right. I watched with interest as we met our allies in the palace of Matsya.
Everyone present here supports you, Yudhishthira, for your cause is just and noble.
I suggest we send a wise man as our messenger to Hastinapur, and persuade Duryodhana to give you your rightful share.
Following Krishna's counsel, my father sent a priest to Hastinapur.
The messenger returned with advice from King Dhritarashtra.
King Dhritarashtra said...
Please remind Yudhishthira that sacrifice is the best virtue.
I expect the Pandavas to give up their desire for any part of the kingdom. They should avoid going to war with my sons.
The message created an uproar.
This is nonsense! Why should we sacrifice our share in the kingdom?
Uncle Dhritarashtra is being foolish! We will not give up our birthright.
It is clear that Duryodhana has complete control over the blind king. We will have to go to war to get back Indraprastha.
I had long since realised that our lives had become a joke for the royals of Hastinapur.

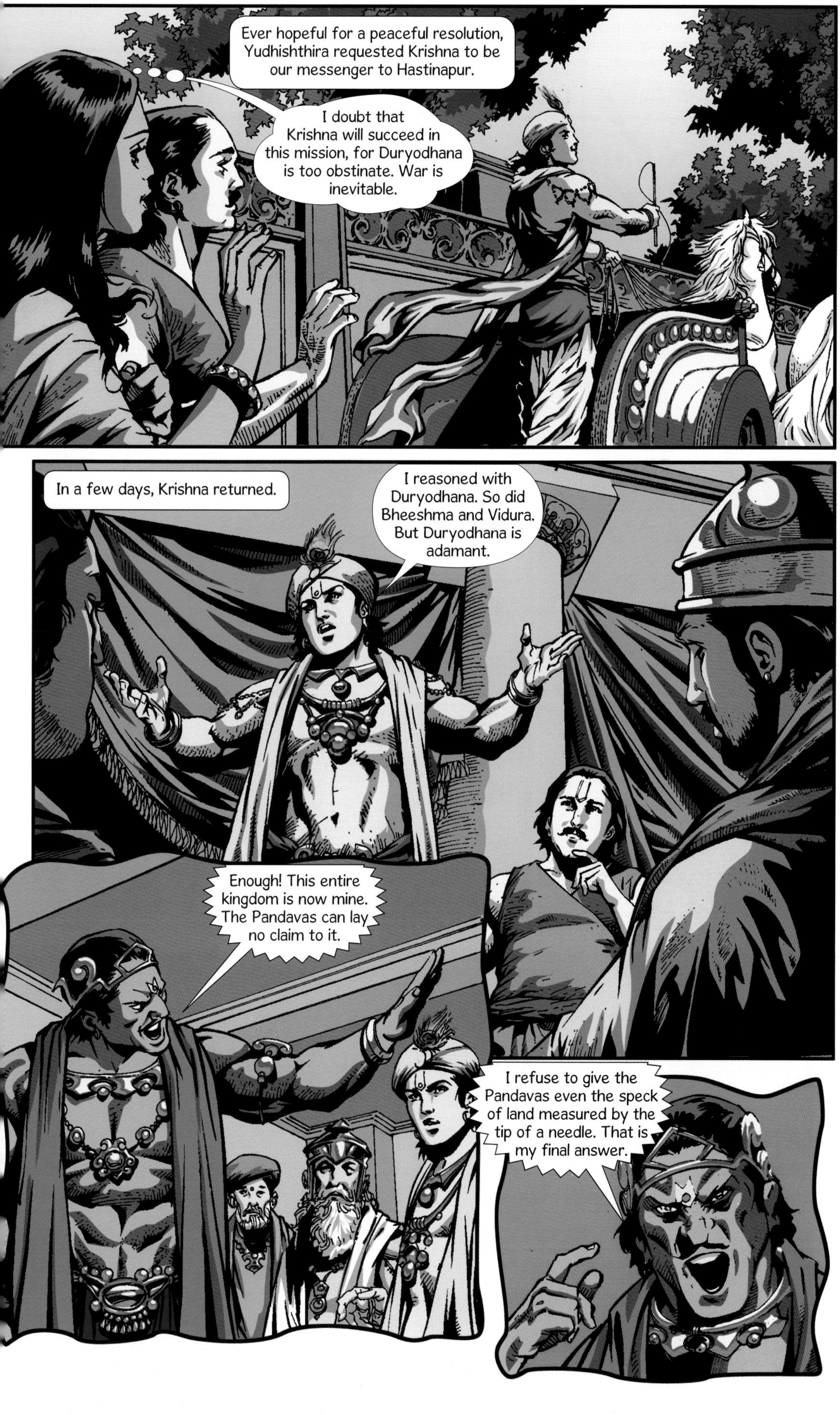

Ever hopeful for a peaceful resolution, Yudhishthira requested Krishna to be our messenger to Hastinapur.
I doubt that Krishna will succeed in this mission, for Duryodhana is too obstinate. War is inevitable.
In a few days, Krishna returned.
I reasoned with Duryodhana. So did Bheeshma and Vidura. But Duryodhana is adamant.
Enough! This entire kingdom is now mine. The Pandavas can lay no claim to it.
I refuse to give the Pandavas even the speck of land measured by the tip of a needle. That is my final answer.

I noticed how Bheema clenched his fists when he heard Duryodhana's mocking words...

...how Arjuna's lips quivered with anger at the thought of Duryodhana insulting Krishna...

...how Nakula and Sahadeva both gripped their swords tighter.

I also noticed Yudhishthira's fallen face, and knew the thoughts passing through his mind.

Be a Kshatriya. Fulfil your duty towards your kingdom and your people. Rid the earth of unjust and greedy men.

Must I actually declare war on my cousins and my uncle?

Are we clear then, that we are to go to war with the Kauravas?

Yes, to war.

It was decided. Messengers were sent to gather allies and build an army.

The search for the best soldiers, horses, elephants, chariots, and weapons began. The Pandavas chose my fire-born warrior brother as their leader.

Dhrishtadyumna, from this day onwards, you shall lead the Pandava army as its supreme commander. Guide us to victory.

Finally, the insults to my honour in the Kuru court would be avenged.

Yet, why does my heart feel sad? Can I never be content?

Days passed swiftly, and the armies gathered on the battlefield of Kurukshetra. The Pandava camp stood on the eastern half of the vast grounds.

It was the morning of the first day of battle. In our tent, I performed the rituals befitting a queen.

May victory be yours for you are upholding dharma.

May the sound of your war cry strike terror in the hearts of the enemy.

May your mighty bow protect our honour and our men.

May you fight with the strength of a hundred gods.

May you slay the enemy and return to me unharmed.

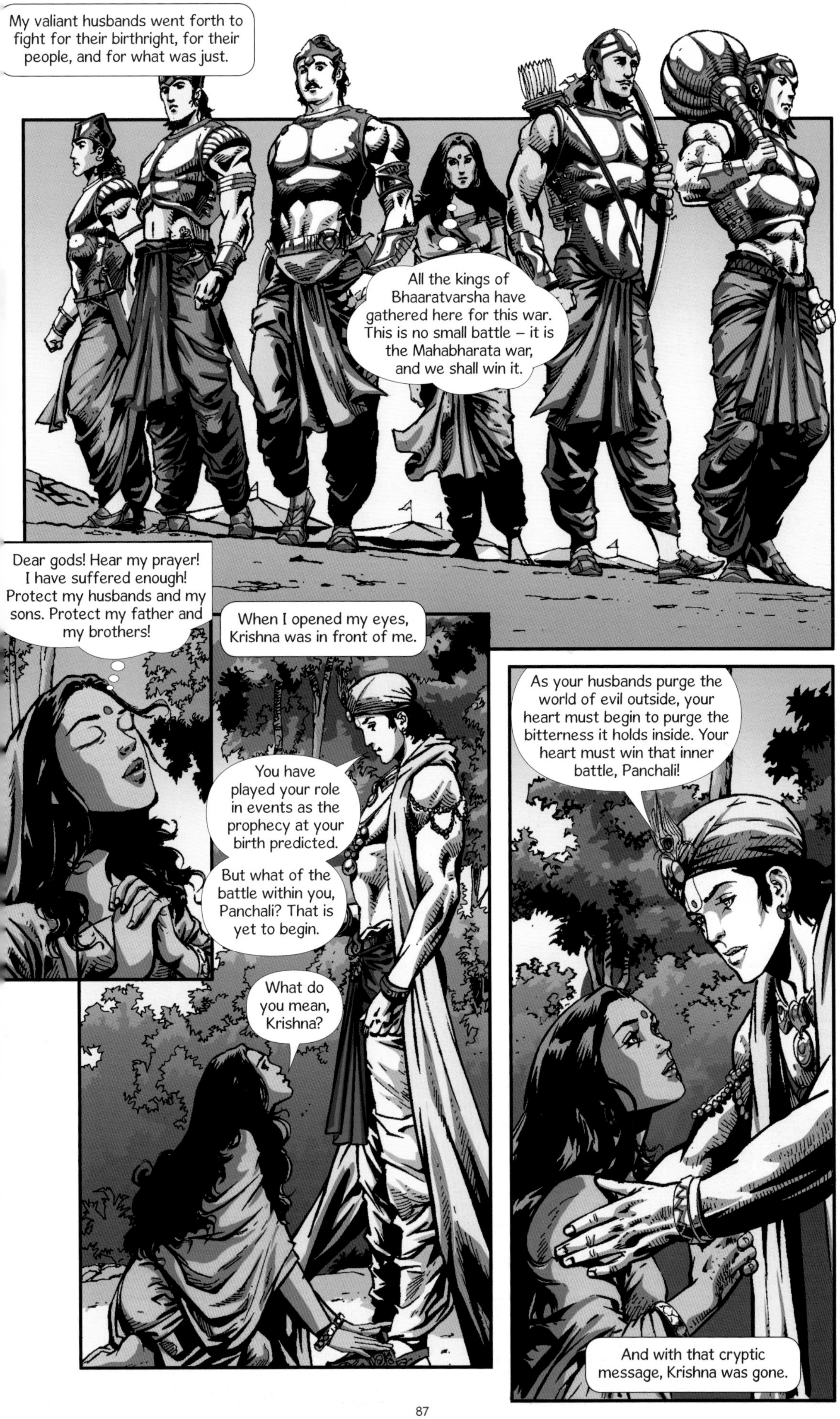
My valiant husbands went forth to fight for their birthright, for their people, and for what was just.
All the kings of Bhaaratvarsha have gathered here for this war. This is no small battle – it is the Mahabharata war, and we shall win it.
Dear gods! Hear my prayer! I have suffered enough! Protect my husbands and my sons. Protect my father and my brothers!
When I opened my eyes, Krishna was in front of me.
You have played your role in events as the prophecy at your birth predicted.
But what of the battle within you, Panchali? That is yet to begin.
What do you mean, Krishna?
As your husbands purge the world of evil outside, your heart must begin to purge the bitterness it holds inside. Your heart must win that inner battle, Panchali!
And with that cryptic message, Krishna was gone.

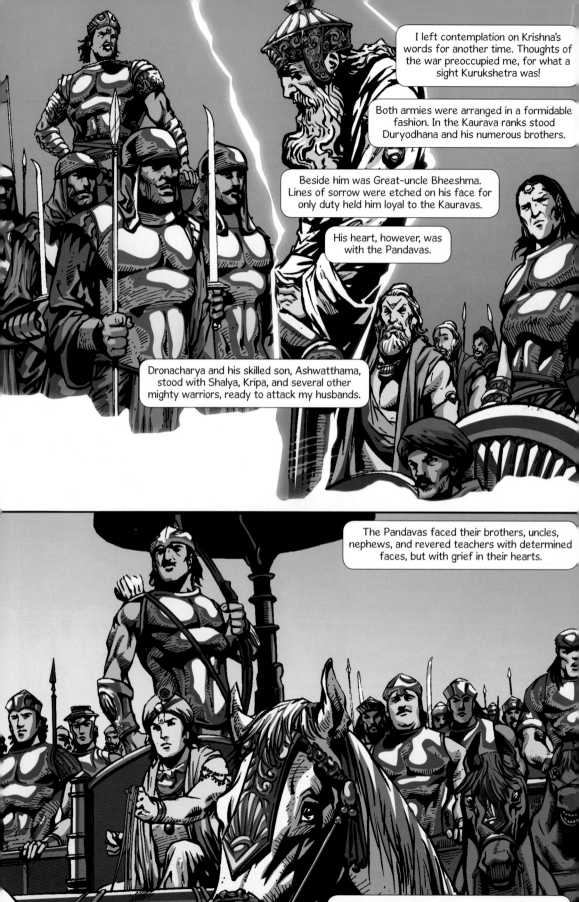

I left contemplation on Krishna's words for another time. Thoughts of the war preoccupied me, for what a sight Kurukshetra was!

Both armies were arranged in a formidable fashion. In the Kaurava ranks stood Duryodhana and his numerous brothers.

Beside him was Great-uncle Bheeshma. Lines of sorrow were etched on his face for only duty held him loyal to the Kauravas.

His heart, however, was with the Pandavas.

Dronacharya and his skilled son, Ashwatthama, stood with Shalya, Kripa, and several other mighty warriors, ready to attack my husbands.

The Pandavas faced their brothers, uncles, nephews, and revered teachers with determined faces, but with grief in their hearts.

Krishna refused to wield a weapon. Instead, he offered to become Arjuna's charioteer, guiding him through the battlefield, and offering him words of advice at crucial moments during the war.

The sound of conch shells rang through the morning air, and I heard the thundering of thousands of galloping horses as the armies charged across the battlefield.

The clang of clashing swords and maces echoed repeatedly while countless arrows whistled as they whizzed through the sky.

Elephants trumpeted, and the war cries of men and animals rose up in the air and mingled with the smell of dust and blood.

Finally, the sun set, and the warriors returned to their camps. My eyes were moist when I greeted my tired husbands and sons.

Thank you, gods, for keeping them safe today!

But the first day had brought bad news too.

I saw Prince Uttara being carried in.

The charming son of Virata lay lifeless before me. Uttaraa and Subhadra wept uncontrollably.

My beloved brother! You were so young... so young!

When all of this ends, shall I have to weep for my brother too, the way Uttaraa weeps for hers?

I forced that thought out of my mind, but it returned, again and again.

But as Kshatriya women, war was a way of life for us. Subhadra and I would spend the nights tending to the men's wounds. We applied balms and pastes of healing herbs.

Abhimanyu, look at this wound! You must be more careful!

It is nothing, Mother! I do not feel a thing!

Abhimanyu, with his youthful exuberance, allayed our fears to an extent.

Do not worry about him, Subhadra! He is, after all, Arjuna's son!

While we soothed his wounds, he calmed our fragile nerves and managed to bring a smile to our lips.

But as days passed, surrounded by death, I could not pretend to smile anymore.

The Mahabharata was a tragic war, and both sides suffered huge losses. Uncles killed nephews, brothers killed brothers. Blood was spilled every day.

My mornings were filled with terror whilst I waited for the safe return of my family and my people. The nights were heartbreaking as I watched them trudge home, exhausted.

I aged more in those eighteen days than I had in the thirteen years of exile.

On the tenth day of the battle, Great-uncle Bheeshma fell.

Arjuna cried as he shot his own great-uncle. But they say Bheeshma welcomed his arrows and forgave him. Great-uncle had a boon that he would choose his moment of death; so Arjuna's arrows did not kill him. He lay there on the battlefield till much after the end of the war, when he finally chose to welcome death.

I cannot even imagine Great-uncle Bheeshma defeated. This war is tearing our family apart!

Great-uncle Bheeshma is a hero, Subhadra! Alas! That he chose to side with the Kauravas!

But that was not the end of it. The thirteenth day of the Mahabharata went down in history as the blackest day ever...

The rule of combat says that one man should fight another. But losing all sense of honour, the Kauravas broke this timeless code of war.

Six Kaurava warriors, including Dronacharya and Karna, surrounded and mercilessly attacked the sixteen-year-old Abhimanyu.

Young and alone, Abhimanyu did his best to counter their onslaught. But there were too many skilled Kshatriyas against him.

Abhimanyu's handsome form hit the ground, and the Kaurava ranks shamelessly celebrated this crime.

After sundown, Subhadra, the widowed Uttaraa, and I made our way through the bloody field towards his body.

The stench of death is unbearable!

When we found him, Uttaraa and Subhadra's lamenting sobs tore through the night.

First my brother, now my husband is dead! My poor, unborn child will never see his father!

Those were not men – they were wolves who attacked my son. Arjuna will avenge my Abhimanyu's death!

Even I, who had been bravely holding back my tears all these days, finally broke down and cried softly.

Abhimanyu! You were dearer to me than my own sons.

All this death and destruction. So many lives lost.

I desired this battle for it would avenge the insults heaped on me many years ago. But this war is not just killing the men I hate. It is also killing the men I love.

Krishna! Have I made a huge mistake by pushing my husbands to choose this war? Or was I just fulfilling the prophecy at my birth?

As Krishna had predicted, my inner battle had begun.

Though troubled by my own questions, I comforted the devastated Uttaraa.

Abhimanyu is at peace, and is now in heaven. Your son will be known as the child of a great hero – the bravest man who ever lived.

Blazing with anger at the cruel death of his son, Arjuna sought revenge.

It was Jayadratha, who had kidnapped me in the twelfth year of exile. Here too, Jayadratha had been responsible for preventing the Pandava army from helping Abhimanyu in his last battle.

Arjuna wasted no time. Under Krishna's skilful guidance, Jayadratha's head was severed from his body.

And another woman, Dushala, was widowed.

It was the fifteenth day of the battle. Dronacharya had now taken command of the Kaurava forces, and he was merciless with the Pandava soldiers.

Drona is using divine weapons on common soldiers. That is against the rules!

I can never forget that he was instrumental in killing Abhimanyu. We have to destroy him.

According to Krishna's plan, Bheema killed an aggressive war elephant named Ashwatthama in the Kaurava battalion. Ashwatthama was also the name of Dronacharya's son.

Krishna persuaded Yudhishthira to tell a half-truth.

But I cannot lie to--

You do not have to lie. You have to tell him 'Ashwatthama is dead'. He will think that you mean his son is dead.

Tell me, Yudhishthira – I fear for my son – I can hear Bheema shouting victoriously that he has killed Ashwatthama. Is this true?

Yes, Ashwatthama is dead.

Ashwatthama the elephant is dead.

But Dronacharya did not hear Yudhishthira's whisper. As Krishna had predicted, he was paralysed with grief at the news of his son's death.

Dronacharya decided to enter a state of deep meditation so that he could shed his body at will. He closed his eyes and stilled his mind. The sounds of the battle vanished for him.

Dhrishtadyumna realised that if Dronacharya heard that his son was alive, he would curse the Pandavas and annihilate their entire army.

Seizing this moment to fulfil his destiny, my fire-born sibling unsheathed his sword and decapitated Dronacharya.

Dhrishtadyumna's eyes shone with light as he understood, in the depths of his soul, that his purpose on earth had been achieved.

Some say that my brother committed a sinful act by killing a meditating Brahmin. Yet others applaud him for avenging Abhimanyu's death and regrouping the scattered Pandava army.

But like me, perhaps, Dhrishtadyumna had no choice in the matter. Our fates were predestined. He was born from the flames to kill Drona, and so he did.

When Ashwatthama heard of his father's death, he took a terrible oath.

The Pandavas will suffer for this! I will avenge the death of my father.

After Dronacharya's death, the Pandavas had the clear advantage. They wasted no time in fulfilling the oaths they had taken in the Kuru court several years ago.

Bheema killed Dushasana – the man who had tried to disrobe me in the court of Hastinapur...

...and brought his blood in a golden goblet to me.

Draupadi, why do you cry? Is this not what you wanted?

Do not ask me that, beloved Bheema. Let me now fulfil my vow!

While my heart and my pride battled each other, I bathed my black tresses in Dushasana's blood...

...and braided my hair for the first time in thirteen years.

But my soul was now troubled by the pain I had caused another queen...

Queen Gandhari must be shattered to hear that Dushasana, too, is dead. Why does my revenge cause so much grief to so many women?

I wrestled with my conscience every single moment. All I wanted now was for the war to end.

96

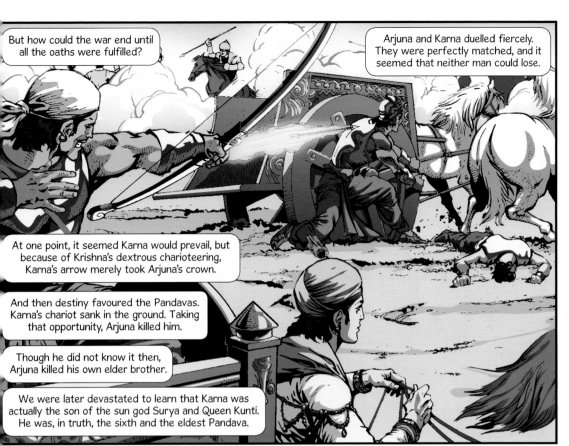

But how could the war end until all the oaths were fulfilled?

Arjuna and Karna duelled fiercely. They were perfectly matched, and it seemed that neither man could lose.

At one point, it seemed Karna would prevail, but because of Krishna's dextrous charioteering, Karna's arrow merely took Arjuna's crown.

And then destiny favoured the Pandavas. Karna's chariot sank in the ground. Taking that opportunity, Arjuna killed him.

Though he did not know it then, Arjuna killed his own elder brother.

We were later devastated to learn that Karna was actually the son of the sun god Surya and Queen Kunti. He was, in truth, the sixth and the eldest Pandava.

Meanwhile, Nakula found Uluka, the son of Shakuni, and killed him.

Sahadeva could never forget that Shakuni had hatched the plan to use the game of dice to send the Pandavas into exile.

Shakuni met his end at the hands of Sahadeva.

The last oath was honoured when Bheema and Duryodhana duelled. Both were agile and adept at wielding the mace.

CLUNG!

The duel lasted long. Krishna and Arjuna watched anxiously. It seemed as if Duryodhana was the stronger of the two.

Bheema needs to be reminded of Duryodhana's words to Draupadi.

Krishna waited till he caught Bheema's eye. Then he patted his left thigh as a cue.

THWACK!

Bheema remembered that gesture of Duryodhana. And he also remembered his own words...

I swore to break your thighs, Duryodhana. Take that!

ARRRGGH!

Duryodhana lay broken on the dusty ground, and died a slow, painful death. With their leader fallen, the Kaurava army disbanded.

Today I have avenged Draupadi's insult. The earth is rid of the Kauravas. No woman shall suffer as she did.

The Mahabharata war had lasted full eighteen days. True to their word, my husbands had slain the hundred sons of Dhritarashtra and Gandhari.

Only three warriors remained in the Kaurava camp, one of whom was Ashwatthama.

The bitter poison of revenge coursed through Ashwatthama's veins. Though the war was over, he was determined to single-handedly cause the Pandavas grief.

My heart was heavy with the death I saw all around me.

The Mahabharata war is over; the earth is rid of evil. What you were born to cause, has occurred. Be at peace now.

We could not have done it without your grace, Krishna.

I only did my duty, Panchali, as you did yours.

I then went to Yudhishthira.

I wish to thank you for staying true to your word, and being a Kshatriya.

But look at the destruction I have caused. My heart is unhappy, Draupadi!

The Kauravas reaped what they sowed. Do not take the burden of guilt upon your shoulders.

THE CONSEQUENCES

As per tradition we slept the first night of peace not in our own camp, but in the abandoned Kaurava camp. My brother and my sons decided to stay back in the Pandava camp.

Thirsting for revenge, in the dead of night, Ashwatthama entered the tent where Dhrishtadyumna slept.

Those Pandavas think they can get away with victory? I will show them. I will do what the entire Kaurava army could not.

With the stealth of a cat, Ashwatthama took his revenge. May no mother ever have to see what I saw after Ashwatthama was done.

Coward that he was, Ashwatthama then fled the camp.

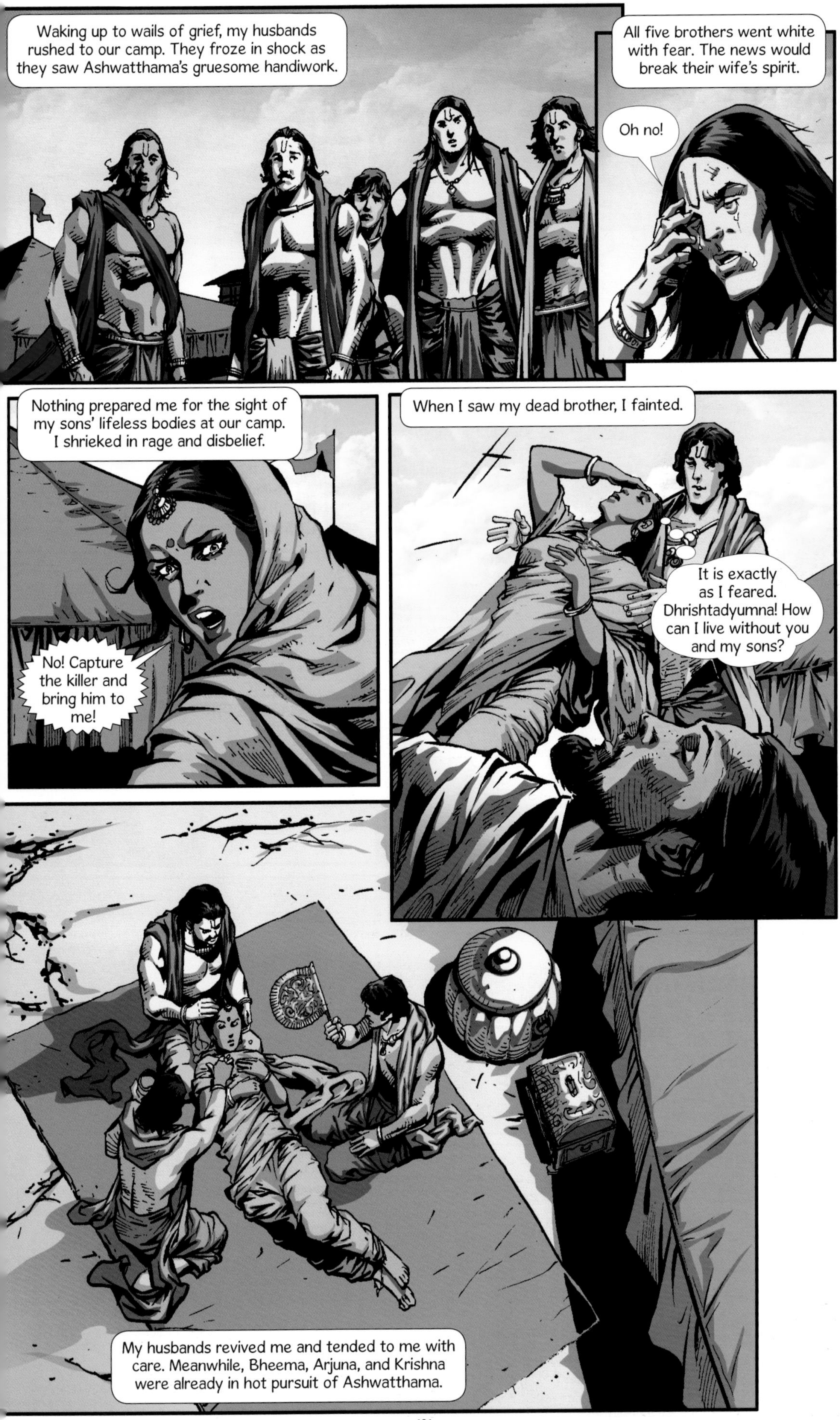
Waking up to wails of grief, my husbands rushed to our camp. They froze in shock as they saw Ashwatthama's gruesome handiwork.
All five brothers went white with fear. The news would break their wife's spirit.
Oh no!
Nothing prepared me for the sight of my sons' lifeless bodies at our camp. I shrieked in rage and disbelief.
No! Capture the killer and bring him to me!
When I saw my dead brother, I fainted.
It is exactly as I feared. Dhrishtadyumna! How can I live without you and my sons?
My husbands revived me and tended to me with care. Meanwhile, Bheema, Arjuna, and Krishna were already in hot pursuit of Ashwatthama.

In a short while, they dragged in Dronacharya's son and threw him at my feet.

This man killed my sons in their sleep, like a coward. He deserves to die!

Here he is, Draupadi. The murderer! Do with him what you will. One word from you, and I shall sever his head.

Strange is the power of destiny. Here I was, finally given the chance to punish a criminal who had made me suffer...

Yet, when I looked into Ashwatthama's eyes, I changed my mind.

Dronacharya's wife is already widowed. The grief of seeing her son dead will tear her apart. I have just suffered the loss of my sons. I know what that grief is...

Incredibly, my inner battle had finally ended.

At that moment, I realised that death and destruction were futile. Revenge solved no problems, and gave no lasting peace.

To learn to forgive is a difficult lesson indeed, and you have learnt it, Panchali. Your heart has won!

Ashwatthama is a free man. I cannot subject his mother to the same pain that I am feeling right now.

I am proud of you, Draupadi. You have the strongest heart of us all.

But for Ashwatthama's cowardly act, Krishna cursed him to roam the earth for three thousand years, and Arjuna ripped off the jewel that was his source of power, from his head.

We travelled to the holy river Ganga where we prayed and performed rituals for those who had died in the war.

I offered prayers for Dhrishtadyumna, Abhimanyu, and my sons. I wept for all those who had to perish so that justice could be won.

I cried for all the women who had been widowed, mothers whose sons had died, and children who had been left fatherless after the war.

My heart aches for the loss of life...

...but the earth is rid of evil. For this, I am grateful.

Most of all, I thanked the gods for I now released the bitterness I had carried through the years of exile.

The prophecy heard at the time of my birth from the sacrificial fire had been fulfilled. The destruction of evil Kshatriyas had been achieved.

My flaming anger had served its purpose. It was finally doused that day, as I, a fire born, drenched myself in the waters of the river Ganga.

Sorrowed by the death of his hundred sons, Dhritarashtra lost all desire to rule the kingdom. He gave up the throne to Yudhishthira.

Take hold of the reins of the kingdom, my son.

Ever respectful, Yudhishthira ensured that Dhritarashtra and Gandhari lived a comfortable life in their palace.

The surrounding kingdoms were now ruled by the sons and nephews of great warriors who had died in the war.

These young princes readily acknowledged Yudhishthira as their supreme leader.

With the help of his brothers, Yudhishthira performed the *ashwamedha* yajna.

Yudhishthira was proclaimed the unequalled emperor.

Long live our king!

Long live our queen!

Yudhishthira and I were then crowned emperor and empress.

Our rule would usher in a new age of prosperity and happiness in Bhaaratvarsha.

The Pandavas and I had a mighty task ahead of us. After the great war, it was time to consolidate and rebuild.

We revived the spirits of the citizens. Clothes and food were distributed. Fields were tended.

Thank you, Your Majesty.

Crops were harvested. Widows and their children were given special care. Life slowly returned to normal.

The Pandavas' and Kauravas' sons had all perished in the war. But Uttaraa carried in her womb the one remaining hope for the Kuru legacy.

She gave birth to Abhimanyu's son. This grandson of Arjuna was named Parikshit.

I was overjoyed to hold a grandchild in my arms, and blessed the little boy with all my heart.

I had missed the most important years of my children's lives. But I was able to relive them through Parikshit's childhood.

Parikshit grew to be as wise as his great-uncle Yudhishthira, as handsome as his father, Abhimanyu, and as brave as his grandfather, Arjuna.

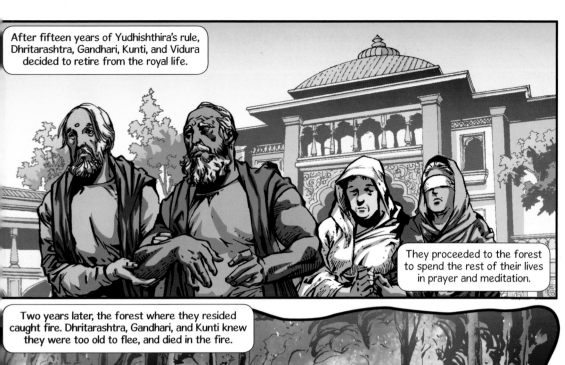

After fifteen years of Yudhishthira's rule, Dhritarashtra, Gandhari, Kunti, and Vidura decided to retire from the royal life.

They proceeded to the forest to spend the rest of their lives in prayer and meditation.

Two years later, the forest where they resided caught fire. Dhritarashtra, Gandhari, and Kunti knew they were too old to flee, and died in the fire.

Not much later, Vidura also passed away.

We were grief-stricken to hear of these deaths, and mourned them deeply.

But time is the great reaper. In the thirty-sixth year of our reign, we were informed of Krishna's death.

It felt as if our hearts had been broken in two.

Arjuna was inconsolable.

Nooo!

And I? My world was shattered. My best friend, my companion, my saviour – Krishna – had left the earth!

With him, a part of all of us died too.

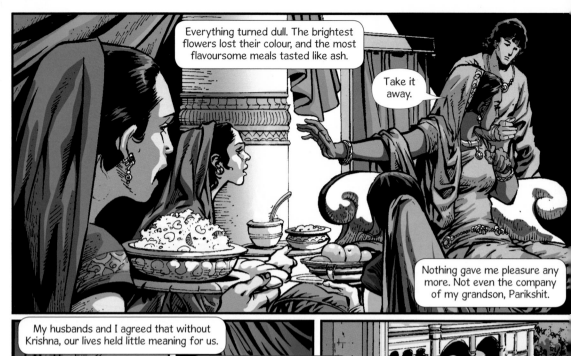

Everything turned dull. The brightest flowers lost their colour, and the most flavoursome meals tasted like ash.

Take it away.

Nothing gave me pleasure any more. Not even the company of my grandson, Parikshit.

My husbands and I agreed that without Krishna, our lives held little meaning for us.

Soon, Parikshit was raised to the throne of Hastinapur. We were confident that Parikshit would make a just ruler, and he did.

After much discussion, my husbands and I abandoned our royal robes, jewels, and weapons, and once again donned the simple garb of hermits.

We decided to proceed on the mahaprasthana – the final journey. It was considered a worthy way to die, and none but the most righteous could achieve it.

The journey meant walking north to the sacred Himalayas barefoot without stopping and without turning back.

We would walk until we eventually dropped dead.

And so I come back to where my story began. The five men who walk ahead of me are my husbands.

I am the first to collapse from exhaustion...

...and tumble over the side of the path, and lie in the cold, wet snow.

My breathing is ragged on that icy slope, and I cannot call out loud enough for help.

Even if I do, there will be no help as the rule of the mahaprasthana says that no one shall turn back. I am alone again.

I hear scuffling sounds. Someone has returned. It is my beloved Bheema.

He weeps as he holds my hand, comforting me.

My lips are frozen, but I whisper a gentle farewell to Bheema, asking him to continue his journey...

...and reminding him that we will meet in the heavenly realm where great warriors reside.

He leaves reluctantly.

I smile as I realise that to say I lived a lonely life is a lie.

For of the five brothers, Bheema had loved and cared for me with all his heart. Even until the very end.

My body grows numb with cold, and I will only breathe a few more breaths of the icy air.

I cannot see my husbands in the distance anymore.

I shiver in the chilly wind and search for the strength that lies deep within my soul.

Aware that I have only a few more moments to live, I fix my mind on Krishna. A great peace fills my heart.

Thanking the gods for the fulfilment of my life's purpose, I let out my last breath.

Light. Brilliant light shines through me. I am ageless again.

And I smile as I am welcomed into the next realm by my eternal friend... Krishna.

The Many Facets
of
Draupadi

The Woman

Draupadi is the most prominent female character in the Mahabharata. She is portrayed as a woman of captivating beauty with a strong and fiery personality. It is Draupadi who persuades her husbands, the Pandava brothers, to avenge her humiliation by their cousins, the Kauravas, which leads to the monumental war of the Mahabharata. Its author is traditionally said to be the great sage, Vyasa. At its core, it tells the story of the Pandava brothers and their struggle against the Kauravas. Not only are they deprived of their kingdom, they are also forced to wander for thirteen years after bitter humiliation at the hands of the Kauravas. All this culminates in the Kurukshetra war that lasts eighteen days.

Draupadi's friendship with Krishna has a special function in the epic. Krishna is said to be an *avatar*, or incarnation, of the Hindu god Vishnu. Throughout the story of the Mahabharata, he advises the Pandavas on various matters at times of peace and war. He is aware of the inevitability of the outcome of the Mahabharata war, and he guides the Pandavas and Draupadi as they play their roles in vanquishing evil.

Legend has it that during a festival, Krishna cut his little finger trying to break sugarcane. When Draupadi saw drops of blood dripping from Krishna's finger, she hurriedly tore a piece of her own garment and wrapped it around his finger. This act of kindness touched Krishna, and he promised that when the time came, he would repay manifold each thread of the piece of cloth wrapped around his finger. When Dushasana attempted to disrobe Draupadi after her eldest husband Yudhishthira lost her in a game of dice, she called out to Krishna for help, and he kept his promise.

Draupadi earned herself many names because of the many facets of her being. As King Drupada's daughter, she was named Draupadi. As princess of Panchala, she was given the name Panchali. Her dusky skin, long black hair, and deep devotion to Krishna earned her the name Krishnaa. As the grand-daughter of Prishata, she was known as Parsati. The name Yajnaseni was given to her because she was born from a yajna (fire ritual) and probably also because of her fiery character. She was also called Mahabharati, great wife of the five descendants of Bharata.

The Goddess

A commanding woman who never hesitated to speak her mind, Draupadi is also worshipped by many as a goddess. A number of temples in South India are dedicated to her. There are around four hundred Draupadi temples in Tamil Nadu and Pondicherry alone. The Draupadi Amman (Mother Draupadi) festival brings communities together in the worship of Draupadi as a village goddess, with unique rituals. One such ritual involves walking on burning coal in honour of Draupadi, who is said to have walked on fire to prove her purity in the Tamil version of the Mahabharata.

The Legend

A wife with more than one husband is not a matter of legend. The practice of polyandry still exists in many villages and communities across India. In the Himalayan regions of Ladakh, Himachal Pradesh, and Uttarakhand, polyandry exists in some degree even today. It is also found among the Todas of the Nilgiris in southern India and the Nishi community of Arunachal Pradesh. Polyandry ensures that land and property remain in the same family. Even in states like Haryana and Madhya Pradesh, the dwindling population of women in recent years has led to more people practising polyandry. Interestingly, the Pandavas are worshipped in a lot of places where polyandry exists.

Dharma

The Indian concept of dharma is difficult to translate into English, as its meaning spans the broad range from righteousness to social order. Dharma can be said to be the code of righteous conduct laid down by ancient texts. These laws or codes ensure that society functions in order. As a member of the warrior caste, a Kshatriya's dharma, for instance, is to protect his kingdom and his people.

Yajna

A yajna is a fire ritual in which priests invoke the blessings of the gods by chanting and pouring offerings into a fire. In the course of our story of Draupadi, three yajnas are mentioned. They are the rajasuya yajna, the vaishnava yajna, and the ashwamedha yajna. The rajasuya yajna was performed by a king seeking the allegiance of other kings and the right to be called supreme emperor. The Pandava king Yudhishthira successfully performed a rajasuya yajna after he set up capital in the city of Indraprashta.

On the other hand, Duryodhana of the Kauravas was also keen on performing the rajasuya yajna, but was prevented from doing so as he was still a crown prince. So he performed the vaishnava yajna instead, proclaiming his invincibility.

At the end of the Mahabharata war, when Yudhishthira was once again proclaimed emperor, he conducted the ashwamedha yajna. This yajna involved a horse being released in the countryside by a king. The wandering horse was followed by an army, and the rulers of all those kingdoms where the horse wandered were supposed to accept the authority of the king performing the yajna, effectively making him emperor. This would last for a year, after which the horse would be sacrificed.

Karna

Karna was the son of Surya, the sun god and Princess Kunti. When Kunti was fourteen, the great sage Durvasa arrived in her father's kingdom. Known to be hot-tempered and hard to please, Durvasa was nevertheless pleased by Kunti's care and attention during his stay. In return, he gave her a powerful mantra by which she could invoke any god to give her a child. Out of curiosity, Kunti chanted the mantra and invoked Surya. True to what Durvasa had said, the sun god gave her a son who was as radiant as himself. Karna was born with a golden armour and earrings on his body. After his birth, Kunti panicked as she was now an unwed mother. Putting the new-born child in a basket, she set him adrift on a river.

Mahaprasthana

Mahaprasthana means the 'final journey' or the 'great departure' where one sets out on his journey towards heaven. A person would continue walking without looking back till his last breath. In the Mahabharata, the Pandavas and Draupadi set out on their final journey towards the Himalayas. On their way, Dharma, the god of righteousness, accompanied them in the guise of a dog.

Shikhandi

The eldest child of King Drupada of Panchala, in his previous incarnation, Shikhandi was the princess Amba, who along with her sisters, was abducted by Bheeshma to be wedded to his half-brother Vichitravirya. She was, however, in love with another king. When Bheeshma took her to him, however, that king refused to marry her. Feeling humiliated and holding Bheeshma responsible for her condition she asked Bheeshma to marry her. Bheeshma declined because of his vow of celibacy. Angry at being rejected, Amba swore to be born a warrior in her next life to avenge the insult.

Shikhandi was instrumental in Bheeshma's fall in the war. He stood in front of Arjuna. Bheeshma could not strike Shikhandi because his code of conduct would not allow him to attack anyone who was not a man. And Arjuna, thus shielded, succeeded in making the great Bheeshma fall.

Niyoga

This was a social practice in ancient India wherein a great sage or a deity could be invoked to grant a child to a woman if her husband was unable to father a child, and so continue the family line. In the Mahabharata, the help of Sage Vyasa was solicited for the birth of Dhritarashtra and Pandu. Also, when Pandu could not have any children of his own due to a curse, his queens, Kunti and Madri, invoked the gods to grant them sons. These sons were called the Pandavas.

Swayamvara

This was an ancient Indian social practice in which a girl of marriageable age could choose a husband from a group of suitors. The father of the bride-to-be would decide the time and place, and on the day of the swayamvara, suitors would assemble, and the bride would make her choice. Sometimes they would be asked to perform certain tasks to prove their skill and excellence, as was the case at Draupadi's swayamvara.

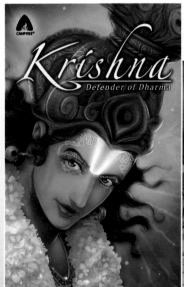